Egypt + 100

ALSO AVAILABLE IN THIS SERIES

IRAQ + 100: Stories from a Century After the Invasion
Edited by Hassan Blasim

PALESTINE + 100: Stories from a Century After the Nakba
Edited by Basma Ghalayini

KURDISTAN + 100: Stories from a Future Republic
Edited by Orsola Casagrande & Mustafa Gundogdu

First published in Great Britain in 2024 by Comma Press.
www.commapress.co.uk

Copyright © remains with the authors, editors, translators and Comma Press, 2024
All rights reserved.

The moral rights of the authors to be identified as the author of this Work have been asserted in accordance with the Copyright Designs and Patents Act 1988.

A CIP catalogue record of this book is available from the British Library.

ISBN-10: 191269770X
ISBN-13: 978-1912697700

This book has been selected to receive financial assistance from English PEN's 'PEN Translates' programme.

The publisher gratefully acknowledges the support of Arts Council England.

Printed and bound in England by Clays Ltd, Elcograf S.p.A

Egypt
+
100

STORIES FROM A CENTURY AFTER TAHRIR

GRAND FORKS
PUBLIC LIBRARY

EDITED BY
AHMED NAJI

Contents

INTRODUCTION — vii
Ahmed Naji
Translated by Majd Abu Shawish

THE WILDERNESS FACILITIES — 1
Mansoura Ez-Eldin
Translated by Paul Starkey

DROWNING — 25
Heba Khamis
Translated by Maisa Almanasreh

EVERYTHING IS GREAT IN ROME — 35
Ahmed El-Fakharany
Translated by Robin Moger

THE MISTAKE — 55
Mohamed Kheir
Translated by Andrew Leber

THE SKY ROOM — 65
Azza Sultan
Translated by Elisabeth Jaquette

ENCOUNTER WITH THE WHITE RABBIT — 75
Michel Hanna
Translated by Mohammed Ghalayini

CONTENTS

THE SOLITUDE OF PRINCE BOUDI Ahmed Wael Translated by Raphael Cohen	91
GOD ONLY KNOWS Belal Fadl Translated by Raph Cormack	99
UNICORN 2512 Nora Nagi Translated by Mayada Ibrahim	111
MAMA Camellia Hussein Translated by Basma Ghalayini	123
ORAL HISTORY OF A PAST, OBSOLETE AND FORGOTTEN Yasmine El Rashidi	129
THE TANTA WHITE PEOPLE MUSEUM Ahmed Naji Translated by Rana Asfour	137
About the Authors	155
About the Contributors	158

Introduction

HERE IS A RIDDLE FOR YOU. Is science fiction...

(i) a perception of the future that stems from current reality or scientific theory; a world that differs from our contemporary one but works according to its scientific rules – in other words, as Ursula K. Le Guin puts it, an 'extrapolative' fiction, taking 'a trend or phenomenon of the here-and-now', purifying and intensifying it for dramatic effect, and extending it into the future ('If this goes on, this is what will happen');[1]

(ii) a visualisation of an *alternative* reality, one that exceeds the world as we know it, as bound by physical and mathematical laws;

(iii) a canon of dramatic themes and literary plots which appear regularly in the literatures of the Global North, but which, if they were to appear in the literatures of the Global South, would be called 'magic realism' or 'folklore';

or (iv) defined by 'its orientation towards the use of science and technology, and often a particular focus on the future, as long as the use of science and futurity is an integral part of the drama.'?[2]

Now, here is a short story for you. After all, we're introducing a book of short fiction not taking a test!

In the summer of 2010, two plain-clothed police officers stopped a young man called Khaled Saeed in a cyber cafe in

INTRODUCTION

Alexandria and attempted to search him. When he asked to see their ID to confirm they were police officers, they started beating him up in front of everyone in the cafe. Then, dragging him out, across the road, and into the entrance of the building opposite, they continued their assault, smashing his head against 'the iron door, the steps of the staircase and walls of the building',[3] finally leaving him dead in the doorway.

Torture was, and still is, a deliberate tactic deployed strategically by the Egyptian police. Khaled Saeed was not the first victim, nor will he be the last. However, the reactions to this incident spread quickly and widely enough to include civil liberties organisations and several youth groups who organised themselves with the help of the internet and social media and took to the streets. It didn't take long for protests to multiply, especially after the Ministry of Interior's denial of the accusations; its report stated that Khaled Saeed's death was a result of him swallowing a marijuana package when the policemen approached him.

Six months later, large-scale demonstrations erupted in Cairo and other governorates where millions of Egyptians flooded the streets. Their demands shifted from a retrial of Saeed's murderers and the dismissal of the Minister of Defence to the overthrow of the entire regime.

The demonstrations lasted eighteen days and ended with Mubarak stepping down from his position after more than 30 years as a president without a single free election.

In the quasi-democratic general election that followed, the Muslim Brotherhood's candidate, Mohammed Morsi won by a small margin. He was a metallurgical engineer specialising in developing surfaces suitable for space rockets. As soon as he took power, Morsi issued several authoritarian orders aimed at seizing full control of the country and transforming Egypt into an Islamic emirate in accordance with his Brotherhood's ideology. Demonstrations erupted, this time against him. Unlike previously, the army joined these demonstrations along

INTRODUCTION

with representatives of other regional powers from Arab Gulf states.

The quasi-democratic experience ended with a military coup against the elected president led by General Abdel Fattah El-Sisi. Moreover, the president of the Constitutional Court, Adly Mansour, was appointed as interim president for one year. In an undemocratic election in May 2014 – coming at the end of months of violent crackdowns on protests and questionable turnout figures – El-Sisi won by a suspiciously wide margin (96%). He has remained in power, ruling with an iron fist ever since. El-Sisi believes in myths and oneiromancy (predicting the future though dreams). He rejects feasibility studies and thinks science and education are worthless and unprofitable investments.

One day, during the transition year – when El-Sisi ruled as the Minister of Interior alongside the President of the Constitutional Court, and the streets were plagued with armed conflicts and mini-civil wars between the supporters of the scientist former-president and the dreamer general – Egyptians woke up to news of a very important press conference about to be held by the military that would announce a gift, not just for the Egyptian people but for all humanity.

In this conference, a man wearing military uniform introduced himself as Doctor General Abdel Atty. In his hand, he held a device that looked like a remote control with an antenna. He announced that the military had invented a new technology that could discover hepatitis, AIDS and other viral diseases in patients without running any tests. To put it simply, the antenna would scan the patient and vibrate if they have any of the diseases.

Doctor Abdel Atty confirmed that he was also working on another device to end hepatitis, AIDS and other viral diseases. In front of the nation's press, he explained that the device would break down the virus's protein using radiation. Then, the protein would be turned into food to be consumed by the

INTRODUCTION

patient. In his own words: 'We will take the virus from the patients and give it back to them as Kebab and Kofte, full of nutrition!'

After the announcement, Egypt's civil health institutions fell silent. A few weeks before this press conference, the military had slaughtered more than a thousand Egyptians in the Raba'a Square massacre. In full view of cameras, the military had burned the protesters' tents with the dead bodies alongside them. Since then, the actions of the Egyptian military and police have been characterised by extrajudicial killings of the protesters. Both forces have continued their unlawful killings of civilians, and enforced the disappearances and imprisonment of political opponents for years without trials (not even sham ones). Under this cloud of fear, everyone has kept quiet. Some doctors and university lecturers even publicly applauded the military's invention that could turn viruses into Kebab and Kofte.

At that time, I was working on my third novel, *And Tigers to My Room*. The main character is a physiotherapist who works in a military hospital. One day, she discovers that the touch of her hand has supernatural healing abilities. She then goes on a journey of recovery from her divorce and attempts to understand the reasons behind her sudden powers. Thinking back now, in the light of Dr Abdel Atty's invention, the science fiction I was writing seemed to fall very far short of reality.

What could literary science fiction hope to achieve against a totalitarian regime that took its *real-world* claims straight out of the SF playbook? And it's not just Egypt. From the 'Neom' project in Saudi Arabia to the 'Brain of Egypt' project, Arab dictators express an almost unlimited appetite for the aesthetics of science fiction.[4] It inspires their political fantasies which, in turn, eventually become the citizens' worst nightmares.

How can a science fiction writer even begin to deal with this reality? How can you 'use your imagination' in a reality

INTRODUCTION

where military personalities and doctor-generals go on air and ask you to believe in a device that can catch the vibrations of a virus, break its protein down and ultimately turn it into Kofte? It's a reality where, if you dare to publicly reject their 'science' and 'logic', you may end up being imprisoned or killed. What is 'science' and what is 'fiction' in this reality?

Again, more questions!

Here is a short essay for you, which is meant to be an introduction to this book.

I often think, and this might be an exaggeration, that the linear perception of time is a spine that runs through the linguistic structure of English (and perhaps other Latin languages). In English, each sentence has to locate itself in a specific timeframe. The future, for instance, can be in the form of simple future tense, future continuous tense, future perfect tense or future perfect continuous tense. Therefore, it is quite easy for English writers and critics to consider science fiction as an attempt to predict the future, following Le Guin's definition.

However, in other civilisations, time can be perceived in non-linear ways. It can be a circle, for instance, where every end/death is a transformation into a beginning/birth. Or, it could be a space where the past, present and future mix together; The Isra'a (the Prophet Muhammad's night journey to Jerusalem) and the Mi'raj (his ascension to heaven) in the Islamic tradition are clear examples.

Following the death of the Prophet Mohammed's first wife and his uncle, he is overwhelmed with a great sadness. One night, he finds Al-Buraq, a winged steed larger than a donkey but smaller than a horse. The Prophet travels to Jerusalem on the back of Al-Buraq. There, he finds all the Prophets who lived and died before his time, waiting for him to lead them in prayer. After the prayer, he ascends with the

INTRODUCTION

archangel Jibril (Gabriel) to the seventh heaven. On his way, he sees people being tortured in hell and others enraptured in heavenly bliss – in what is assumed to be in the future, following Judgment Day. Finally, he returns to his bed before the sheets even get cold.

In the linear perception of time, this story is considered impossible. It even lacks any logical narrative. However, from an Islamic point of view, time is a place where humans live. God and his angels, on the other hand, live outside this place. Therefore, God has the power to see the past, present and future all at once, no matter the actions or choices of humans trapped inside time. With his infinite power, God can bring all the Prophets of the past together alongside the bliss of the heaven which is the future that's supposed to come after doomsday and the end of time. And yet, after all this, on the same night, the Prophet Mohammed is able to return to his bed before it gets cold.

This perception of time, particular to Arab culture, is reflected in Egyptian science fiction. One of the pioneering literary works in the genre is Yousef Izz El-Din's story, 'Wheel of Days', published in 1939. It starts with a scene of an old couple gazing at the sunset. They notice that the sun is moving east not west and the wheel of time is going backwards; yesterday becomes tomorrow; the moment of birth becomes the moment of death; and the past becomes the future. If we put this story on Le Guin's spectrum, we would not be able to locate it in any particular moment, past or future, and would therefore struggle to classify it as science fiction.

In the early days of Egyptian science fiction, this clash between Western (or European) perceptions of time and the Islamic perception of it became very apparent. From this contradiction, the first wave of science fiction was born, such as the work of Tawfiq Al-Hakim (1898-1987). An example of this is his novel *People of the Cave* which takes its inspiration from the Islamic myth of the Seven Sleepers, where a group of youths go to sleep in a cave and wake up some 300 years later.

Another example is the novel *The Conqueror of Time* by Nihad Sherif (1932-2011). The novel follows the life of a rich doctor who discovers a scientific method to freeze the human body for decades until such a time as humanity can finally defeat all diseases and achieve immortality. Then, he will bring himself back to life along with the people he chooses to live with in this eternal future. Nihad Sherif gave his life to science fiction. First coming to prominence in the sixties, he worked primarily as a journalist specialising in science reporting for the *Akhbar Al-Youm* newspaper. He also worked as an advisor to Gamal Abdel Nasser's governments advising on several ministerial projects such as the 'typical village' project and the 'Al-Tahrir Governorate'. These ambitious schemes strove to develop a new concept for the village and agricultural society more generally within a socialist framework designed to educate farmers and improve their lives through creating 'planned villages' as a futuristic model of how rural societies could be.

The 1967 war put a stop to these projects as well as the wider project of national liberation and reform initiated by Abdel Nasser. However, in the seventies, a new generation of science fiction writers emerged, writers like Dr. Mustafa Mahmoud, Rauof Wasfi and Sabri Mousa. Furthermore, science fiction motifs became an integral part of the mosaic of modern Egyptian literature, being used even by writers who did not regard themselves, or their work, as science fiction such as Gamal Al-Ghitani (1949-2015) in the novel *The Roaming of the City* and Yousif Al-Sibaei (1917-1978) in *You Are Not Alone*.

The real explosion of science fiction, however, and its transformation into a popular form of literature, started in the eighties when the Modern Arab Association invited Arab writers who were interested in the genres of SF, horror and crime to submit manuscripts. The Association had started life

INTRODUCTION

as a publishing house specialising in educational books, but in 1983, it launched the first book in its new youth-oriented 'Malaf Al Mostakbal' ('Future File') series, by novelist Nabil Farouk (1956-2020). The events of these novels take place in the future following the adventures of an Egyptian scientific intelligence team; more than a hundred novels were published in this series. Farouk wrote mainly adventure books and one-off novels focusing on crime and science fiction. Patriotism characterised most of his work – his heroes were predominantly intelligence officers, or brave, quick-thinking men.

In the early nineties, many writers joined Farouk in this field; authors such as Mohammed Suleiman Abdul Malek, Raouf Wasfi, and Dr. Ahmed Khaled Tawfik (1962-2018). Tawfik became the best-selling and most influential of these writers in the decades that followed, so much so that he became known as the 'Godfather of Arab Science Fiction'.

Millions of copies of these Modern Arab Association books were sold across the Arab world. The Association had generated a huge appetite for genre fiction. But their works stayed well within conservative conventions and never raised questions about issues such as gender, sex, religion or politics. On the contrary, they were full of nationalist rhetoric and reactionary moral principles. Since he was targeting the youth, Tawfik as well as other writers took care to neutralise any ideas that might cause concern.

Only in the last decade of his life did Tawfik free himself from the Modern Arab Association's editorial polices. He began publishing novels targeting older readers, with his main theme being dystopia. His most famous novel from this time, *Utopia*, envisions a future Egypt where the rich live in gated communities surrounded by high walls. The poor are never allowed to enter these communities and instead have to occupy a miserable reality ruled by ignorance and pollution – a life without science, education or health, based only on talismans and supplication.

INTRODUCTION

Tawfik published *Utopia* in 2008. Three years later, in 2011, the January 25th Revolution erupted followed in 2013 by the June 30th military coup – five years after the novel was published. Currently, El-Sisi is building a new capital – the New Administrative Capital – in the heart of the desert, surrounded by a huge wall, as well as a moat to prevent anyone from even getting to the wall. Moreover, Egyptians would need tickets and special permits to enter the new capital.

Against this backdrop, the number of Egyptian writers exploring genre writing has exploded, especially horror and science fiction. These are either writers who specialise in the genres exclusively or those who see it as as an integral part of their toolbox. In this selection, we have tried to present a cross-section of writers that showcase the diversity of contemporary Egyptian literature generally, not just science fiction. The theme of the '+100' series has helped us in this regard.

For the project we invited writers well-versed in science fiction (Michel Hanna, Ahmed Al-Fakharani), writers known for literary realism (Nora Naji, Azza Sultan), and other writers known for their political and satirical work (Bilal Fadel). We also considered the geographical diversity of Egyptian writers and where they choose (or are forced) to live: some live in Cairo, others outside the capital, and others have to write in exile. Since Egyptian literature is not only written in Arabic, we also invited Egyptian writers who write in English, like Yasmine El Rashidi, to participate.

All of these writers share the same sense of national identity as well as their involvement, in one way or another, in the January 25th Revolution, which turned their world upside down and rebuilt it once again. We asked all the contributors to imagine the Egypt of January 25th 2011 only a hundred years later – *extrapolated*, as Le Guin would say, but based on a political extrapolation of that moment in time, more than a scientific one. We didn't guide or instruct the writers and only demanded one thing: that all the stories be set a century after the revolution, in January 2111. The result is a series of visions of the future inspired by the dreams and nightmares of the present.

Ahmed Naji
Translated by Majd Abu Shawish

Notes

1. Ursula K. Le Guin in the introduction of her novel *The Left Hand of Darkness*.
2. Barbara Dick (2016) *Modern Arabic Science Fiction: Science, Society and Religion in Selected Texts*, Durham theses, Durham University. Available at Durham E-Theses Online: http://etheses.dur.ac.uk/11907/
3. Mohamed Khalil, interviewed. https://www.youtube.com/watch?v=CH2RDwXZjqg
4. Neom is a $500 billion project to create a new city (complete with 'flying taxis, robotic avatars and holograms'), and a key part of Saudi's 'Vision 2030' to diversify away from the kingdom's oil-dependent economy.

The Wilderness Facilities

Mansoura Ez-Eldin

Translated by Paul Starkey

-1-

IT WAS AN ORDINARY winter's day, with an abundance of clouds that had yet to fulfil their promise of rain, when a woman in her fifties left her home wearing black, loose-fitting clothes. Her head was covered with a transparent chiffon headscarf thrown around it with deliberate neglect. She was on her way to buy the vegetables, bread and meat she needed. The very idea of it seemed strange to her, something belonging to a bygone time, and filled her with a vague excitement. She thought of the reaction of the staff in the shopping centre's various departments when they saw someone going to buy their provisions in person rather than relying on the mechanised delivery services. This made her even more excited. She wanted to see the surprise etched in their eyes; she longed for a reaction that was not canned or preserved and wary, for a change.

She could not have predicted that this simple action would lead to such nasty consequences, and it did not occur to her that every one of her movements was watched after she left the house, especially as she preferred to walk rather than take the public bus, which was divided into separate units, one for each passenger.

She must have looked odd as she walked alone along such a colossal street, lined on both sides by enormous buildings. She looked at the dwarf ficus trees clipped brutally into the shapes of animals and birds along the street's central reservation, and her heart sank despite being used to this sight since her childhood. There must be other types of trees in the world, she thought, that were not dwarf ones or trained in this harsh fashion. Then she swallowed this idea, because she felt that she herself was a dwarf who could hardly have been seen amidst this vast, claustrophobic expanse of giant buildings with elaborate decor and complex ornamentation.

In the commercial centre, she passed through section after section but did not know what she ought to do or choose. She discovered that she was ill-prepared, psychologically, to face the looks of doubt and fear in the eyes before her, or to order what she wanted directly rather than sit at home pressing buttons on a screen. Then she quickly realised that there were no human sales staff in the place, only robots responding to mechanical orders. Confused, she wondered where she ever came up with the idea of humans visiting shops, given that she had never been to one before.

With no prior intention of doing so, she found herself announcing her dissatisfaction with the products on display: she picked up a warm, round loaf of bread and directed her words at the robot standing in the bakery in a voice that combined reproach with humour: 'Is this bread? Do you even know how to bake quality bread?'

The loaves looked tasty and had nothing obviously wrong with them, but she left them and stood in front of the vegetables in the neighbouring section, and raised her voice even more: 'I ask for spinach and you bring me chard. Is this spinach?'

Of course, no one replied, but she got the feeling the robot

THE WILDERNESS FACILITIES

was looking at her as one might a madman. Certainly, it would never have encountered anyone raising their voice in public or showing their anger or protest to others. That was quite apart from the fact that it had never before dealt with people buying their necessities themselves, let alone standing examining the products on display with outright dissatisfaction. For the first time, she felt fearful of the robots, especially those that occupied public spaces. Suddenly they looked just like surveillance devices, whose aim was to monitor every inch of her existence.

After an exasperated tour of the fruit and dessert sections, the woman ran away hysterically, unaware that she had left behind her a battlefield. A large part of her anger was directed at herself, since she didn't understand what had come over her, or what had induced her to behave in such a strange way – or, most importantly, what had changed her, without warning, into someone suffering from a persecution complex.

All she knew was how surprised she still was at her dreams during the previous week. For the last seven nights, she had found herself in places foreign to everything she knew, with crowds of noisy people, markets packed with goods and products, and people buying things only after heated arguments or furtive whispers with the shopkeepers. There were also free-growing trees spreading their branches into the space around them, cafés and spacious restaurants seating dozens of customers, and streets paved with smooth asphalt or stones that didn't slow you down or make those walking on them feel they were struggling to get anywhere.

All this enchanted her, and its spell travelled with her from her sleeping hours to her waking day. She wanted to live in a world like that, and became angry at the architecture around her that dwarfed everyone, at the infatuation with granite, marble and basalt, with the construction fever that had ravaged the city, and the rough stones that paved the surface of the roads just to slow drivers down. In short, she had become fed up with the entire vocabulary of her city. So she resolved to try to live in a world like that of her dreams, even if reality was against her.

She figured that it hadn't started with these nightly visions, it was rather the result of what had happened on her day off just before they began. She had gone out that day, armed with her binoculars, and had taken a bus to the Central Wilderness Facility not far from where she lived. She felt like she, in her own glass compartment of the bus, and the other passengers, in theirs, resembled the inmates in the wilderness facility in many ways, and perhaps this is what weighed on her so much when, half an hour later, she found herself staring at the actual inmates through her binoculars. As usual, she was terrified by the details of the labyrinthine structure, with its never-ending staircases and almost complete absence of walls, the only noticeable walls being the glass ones behind which the convicts slept. But there was nothing usual about the sorrow that had descended on her since her last visit. It was as if an unwelcome guest had taken the place of the earlier contentment that she often felt during this ritual, usually justifying it to herself as gratitude that she wasn't in these people's place.

She put the image of the robots in the shopping centre out of her head and ignored the dwarf ficus trees, the convoys of armoured cars roaming the streets, and the antennae on top of them monitoring things she couldn't even guess at. She tried to imagine alternatives to this network of intersecting roads but her imagination failed her. The most she could do was avoid looking at the identical, hideous memorial statues set up at each major road junction. By the time she got home, she felt choked by her anger. She prepared a quick meal and sat eating, alone as usual. Then, without thinking, she set about getting rid of all the electronic equipment she owned. First she smashed it, then she threw it in the bin.

Next morning, she was found dead in her bed. There was nothing to indicate any struggle on her part, and no sign of violence was found, except for the four stab wounds to her chest from a sharp knife. The sky was cloudy and threatening heavy rain.

THE WILDERNESS FACILITIES

-2-

Shihab stopped his car in front of a five-table café, and asked for a coffee with milk, ignoring the waiter's look of surprise at his traditional order. He preferred this café because the staff there were human. He looked around him and noticed that the counter and the wall behind it, stacked with glasses, resembled a bar, even though there was no alcohol on sale, here, or anywhere else in the vicinity. For decades, anything that dulled the mind or numbed the senses had been forbidden. He was one of the few who knew the reason and the background to these laws. He glanced at the five tables and the carefully calculated distances between them, each one with a single customer sitting at it, unaware of their surroundings, unwilling to communicate with anyone outside their orbit. He congratulated himself on this calm, measured atmosphere, even though he acknowledged secretly that nothing was more conducive to relaxation than cafés and restaurants with five tables, except for those with three tables. What made him happier than anything else was the sight of people in harmony with the new forms of architecture, and not protesting about them.

He knew that when the sun of this giant architecture, with its chessboard planning, first rose, it had been received with widespread protests and described as the architecture of fear. The early pioneers of this tactic were accused of trying to subjugate people by making them feel small and helpless in the face of stone. It took an iron fist to establish this style and banish everything that had gone before. Then new generations appeared who had not known any different and were at ease with it, and even if they hadn't been, they couldn't remember anything else.

Now, there was no need for such brute force, unless it was in the form of swift undercover raids designed to nip in the bud any disruption to the apparent harmony before the general public noticed it. How proud he felt to belong to a dynasty that had introduced this civilised method to societal 'management'. He would not use words like 'control' and 'subjugation', as the rabble might, who'd been exiled to the ruins and wastelands outside the perimeter of their civilised existence, or who'd been confined to the 'wilderness facilities'.

He took his coffee back to his car, ignoring the sudden downpour of rain, and continued his calm tour of the city with its parallel and intersecting streets without a single square. He was informed of the death of 'the shopping centre madwoman', as he called her; he had received reports on what she had done yesterday at the time, as all her movements were observed immediately.

He knew there was no room for any error in this utopia, no room for any cog, no matter how small, to slip out of place. He now had to investigate this murder and release the name of the culprit and his motives. The media were now constantly talking about it, describing the woman as having all the attributes of a model citizen at peace with her environment, and kept republishing photos of her, smiling in front of the enormous edifice that was her workplace that made her look like a tireless, happy ant. There was naturally no indication of the folly she had embarked on the morning before, since it would not be right to sully the biography of someone who could no longer defend themselves or justify their follies. As if anyone would bother to listen, either way. But if this matter were to go public, others might be tempted to follow suit, and God only knows what the consequences of such a slip might be.

Near the military base, with its high, seemingly endless walls, he pulled over, to check his tablet for the latest developments. He always stopped in the same spot, as usual keeping to all the rituals of his daily routine, knowing deep down that this slavish submission to habits would one day land him in trouble. He smiled at the thought, trying to imagine the sort of troubles that might befall a person like him. He shook his head and laughed out loud, then quickly chided himself for it. He reminded himself that ahead of him, or perhaps behind, lay a crime of murder and that he had to feed the public's curiosity around it, provide them with circumstances and motive. Then he laughed again. If there had been anyone watching him on a screen, they would have thought him mad or drunk, but he was completely sober and sane. He watched the rain pouring down after several months of drought and smiled. He remembered he should have visited Dhai the night before, but he had forgotten in the middle of his numerous preoccupations. He felt sorry because he might not be able to pass by her hut today either. He'd planned to pop by that evening, if he'd finished all his duties, or else, reluctantly, he'd have to postpone it till he had the time.

'She'll have to wait,' he said caustically to himself, then drove his car away from the military base. He was conscious that he had racked up a lot of secrets in his time, and thought this was perfectly normal. But the idea that every apparently decent citizen out there might similarly be harbouring a host of secrets themselves made him suddenly quite depressed. Other people's potential secrets, he realised, were his mortal enemy and his job was to reveal them, if they existed, one after the other.

-3-

Fog hung over the wooden hut that stood way outside the conurbation. Not far away, a kingfisher perched on an olive tree, trying to penetrate the veil and see what lay in wait for it. It spied shapes that seemed gelatinous in the morning mist, so it took to the wing. The sun slowly appeared, making the world look a little clearer. As the bird flew higher, the shapes gave way to forests of camphor, gazorina, willow and sycamore trees. From its lofty position, the bird could not see Dhai as she sat staring out of the hut window, or even when she came out to stand in front of the hut and look anxiously down the road. The bird did not know Dhai, and perhaps never would know her, although in this moment one thought united them: hunger.

The bird landed again on the old olive tree, untroubled by its enormous, gnarled trunk, full of holes. Immediately, it noticed the young woman standing like a statue with her back to the hut and the forests, her face turned towards the unpaved road, lined on both sides with milk thistle, wet in heavy dew. When she grew bored of her aimless waiting, Dhai turned around and saw the beautiful bird with its turquoise back and orange breast. She was too preoccupied to examine it closely and even if she had done, she wouldn't have known what it was called, having never seen a kingfisher before, or even imagined that such a beautiful creature could exist. If she had been as cultured and educated as the people in the city, she might have deduced that there was a body of water nearby with fish in it; kingfishers feed on fish so they are found wherever there is water.

Dhai had often envied the inhabitants of the conurbation and wished she could be one. But she came from a family of early rebels who had been banished to the ruins and deprived of all the rights granted to those who were in tune with the new path and worshipped architecture as the highest art form and the dividing line between civilisation and barbarism.

Her parents had passed away during an obscure epidemic that killed most of their neighbours. Her brother was arrested and put in a wilderness facility when he tried to sneak into the city to live; she had got to know Shihab during his investigation of the case. She thought she would end up joining her brother, but Shihab took pity on her. So she didn't object when he moved her to this isolated hut, hoping that he would one day keep his promise to move her to urban life, once she was ready to live there. She couldn't understand why he hadn't visited her the previous evening, knowing that her food had run out and that she would have nothing to eat or drink until he brought something.

She didn't understand him, and she hadn't understood until this moment why he had chosen her in particular. But when she thought about it, she quickly realised she scarcely knew anything about his life in the city, or his past. Perhaps he had a wife and children there, although he had often denied it. When she dared ask him how he was able to move between the world of civilisation and their world without constraint or punishment, he replied to her curtly: 'Because I can! It's that simple!'

She continued standing until the fog had lifted completely and the kingfisher reappeared. Its bright colours, turquoise and orange, delighted her, but her happiness didn't last long, for the sky suddenly clouded over so much that it made Dhai feel a great darkness was about to settle over her world. She took refuge in her hut and, from the window, watched the rain pour down with all the sadness it evoked in her, being forever linked with the memory of her mother's songs, that she always sang when it fell. These songs had never ceased, even during the epidemic that claimed the lives of most of those she knew, living in the ruins, while the city remained so free of it the people in the ruins began to believe it was just a biological war directed against them.

-4-

That same morning, in one of the wilderness facilities situated on the edges of the city – the desert behind it, the suburbs in front, with all their colossal buildings and dwarf trees clipped in the shape of flightless birds and frozen animals – the inmates woke to find the display screens suddenly turned on and realised that something momentous had occurred.

In normal circumstances, inmates would remain completely cut off from the outside world, their screens only ever coming on to tell them about some incident in the facility, usually involving a warning, or rather a threat.

But today, the screens were occupied by the image of a humble woman in her fifties, her eyes lined with traces of chronic depression. Video clips of her followed, from which her voice was absent, replaced instead by a melodious voice-over, praising the woman and bestowing on her all the attributes of the good citizen in the new age: obedience, avoidance of small talk, compliance, diligence at work, and a willingness to inform on those who showed signs of rebellion, however close they were to her.

Immediately after this, a picture was shown of the woman murdered in her bed, her face frozen in terror and shock. Her body was covered in a white cover stained with large pools of blood. There was congealed blood on the floor beside the bed.

It seemed as if someone was enjoying showing the murdered woman for as long as possible in front of frightened eyes. Over the decades, murder had become part of the past, thanks to new methods of punishment and rehabilitation, but here they were, rearing their heads again to frighten even criminals locked up in wilderness facilities. Eventually, the screens were turned off and every inmate headed to one of the points in the building that most resembled a maze. Almost entirely devoid of walls, it was a place packed with ascending and descending stairs, leading to narrow cubes with glass walls and places to sleep; beyond this though, it was open to the winds, which howled through them making the residents of this correctional facility feel exposed the whole time, as well as constantly watched – a feeling only amplified by the glass cells they had to sleep in. It was precisely this that drove many of them to stay for the longest time in narrow, stifling bathrooms, these being the only places where they had some privacy.

All the inmates were disturbed by the sight of death staring at them from the display screens. But one of them shuddered with fear and lost his nerve, running and collapsing in the nearest corner he could find. Only this resident, called The Professor, understood the full dimensions and significance of the situation, and for the first time in a while felt that he had fallen outside of time, left hung out to dry. Although he had been incarcerated here for years, he had never lost the feeling that he belonged to the elite who defined the principles and condition of the game. How could it be otherwise, when it was he who founded the philosophy of the wilderness facilities in the first place, and defined their principles? He invented 'the theory of gentle force'. That he had himself been caught in the very web of threads he'd once helped construct, was merely a superficial detail.

He had long believed that his presence in this place was a passing matter and a mistake that would quickly be rectified, and that he would soon return to his previous position, as the mastermind of the whole operation, with the final say on everything. But after what he had just seen with the others on the display screens, he was no longer certain about anything.

He remembered the moment when the ingenious idea first came to him: huge buildings, almost without walls, filled with holes and gaps that would make anyone inside feel they were outside but without the feeling of comfort associated with the open air. There would be no furniture and the floors would be full of staircases, so that anyone looking at them from outside would feel that they were confronted by a maze of interconnected staircases, scattered between which would be small crevices where the condemned could lie. Only with a pair of binoculars could anyone passing by these buildings be able to see inmates clearly inside. Without them they would look like scattered spots. Despite this, though, the inmates' mental health would still be affected by the suspicion that the whole world was watching them.

The Professor said to himself, as if to persuade an imaginary crowd: Walls are a deception; walls give a sense of security. I don't know who associated them with chains! The controlled outdoors, as I invented it, inflicts the ultimate punishment and loss of security. Ordinary citizens can be trained using walls and tiny housing units inside great buildings. But outlaws and those who spread chaos cannot be deterred except by the fruit of my mind.

He chalked up years in this place, waiting for the moment when Shihab would need him again, concocting scenarios in his mind for how he would behave then. Would he renounce the ideas that had brought him here? Would he pretend to be remorseful and declare that his sanity had been restored? When his fantasies ran away with him, he imagined a scenario in which Shihab apologised to him and acknowledged the validity of what he'd said, and asked him to take his magnificent vision on to the next stage.

Deep down though, he sometimes acknowledged that it wasn't in his interests to voice his ideas or even hint at them in public. He was supposed to be the foremost expert on the current regime. He used to tell himself that it was his right to believe in the superiority of philosophy and reason over architecture. For philosophers and theorists like him were the people who laid the foundations for social control; they were the ones who constructed the doctrine, intellectually. Compared to them, architects and city planners were merely the implementers of that vision! But he should have kept such thoughts to himself. His mistake was that, in bouts of self-aggrandisement, he had started to express his discontent and to preach his ideas in close circles. Most dangerously, he had repeated in front of Shihab nonsense like: 'Ideas have wings, and the mind is the master and leader.' The latter had led him on by asking: 'Whose mind? Whose mind do you mean?'

When The Professor replied contemptuously: 'The human mind, any mind that thinks and invents!' Shihab realised that The Professor had strayed from the path and exposed his arrogance: that having invented the idea of the Wilderness Facilities and laid out the principles of the prevailing philosophy of punishment of the day, he was somehow immune from it.

-5-

While The Professor was contemplating his fate and trying to figure out what Shihab was up to on the outside and what he had planned for him specifically, a man with a sprouting beard, unkempt hair, untidy clothes and bloodshot eyes, was trying to dodge the surveillance networks he knew by heart, to escape from the conurbation. He hadn't slept the previous night, even for a few minutes. He had stayed awake, torn between waiting for whoever would come to take him to one of the wilderness facilities or kill him, as had happened to the poor woman, and fleeing to the ruins outside the urban sprawl. In the end, he chose to flee, to preserve his life.

Yesterday, he had noticed deliberate interference on the surveillance network of a certain district. As an experienced officer responsible for the city's principal surveillance network, he could see that whoever had created this interference knew what they were doing. This agitated him. He considered it a challenge to his abilities, so he cancelled the interference, with both curiosity and a desire to continue watching everything happening around him. Over the years, surveillance had become part of his bloodstream, and he had become skilled at inventing difficult-to-trace methods of monitoring people. But now he wished he had not got involved in the whole business, for among what the screens in front of him had shown, was the terrifying scene of a woman being murdered in her bed. His terror had not derived from the violence and bloody nature of the crime, but from the identity of the killer, who did not bother to hide his face or even send an anonymous hitman to do the job for him.

-6-

Dhai spent every hour of the day hungry. She had had nothing to eat except for a few mushrooms, which she had collected between the nearby trees when the rain had paused for a while. She only devoured enough to stave off her hunger, as she hated mushrooms and only ate them when she had to. She was sad that she hadn't planted the small yard in front of the hut as her mother used to in their hut a long way away. She hadn't brought any seeds with her and doubted whether Shihab would bring her any, even if she begged him. It sometimes occurred to her that it would be to his advantage for her to stay here in constant need of him, but she dismissed the idea whenever it came to her, because believing it meant acknowledging that she had no support or help in this savage world.

The hunger pressing on her nerves and her feeling of failure and abandonment had left her in a state of nostalgia, longing for her past days in their old neighbourhood: 'the land of the savages,' as Shihab called it, not aware, or perhaps not caring, that this description hurt her, and confirmed to her that high walls divided them. She came close to asking him once: 'What are you even doing with a savage?'

Fortunately she swallowed her question at the last moment.

By midnight, Dhai had fallen into a deep sleep, so she didn't notice when Shihab opened the hut door and set down the food he had brought for her in the corner of the kitchen. She only woke when he threw himself on top of her and started to kiss her violently. For the first time, she felt disgusted by his advances, which she put down to hunger and the overwhelming feeling of humiliation that clung to her. She threw him off her and he did not resist. He got up gracefully and lit the kerosene lamp, which made her nervous.

He stayed where he was, in a corner of the hut, while she went over to where he had left the food. She prepared the small table, arranged the food on it, and sat down to eat absentmindedly; he joined her. To stop thinking about what had just happened between them, she told him about the beautiful bird she had seen in the morning, and he told her its name: 'kingfisher'. He added that it lived wherever water could be found because it fed on fish. It occurred to her that this bird was brighter than she was because it could feed itself and not rely on others; then she started to imagine a possible body of water nearby. She felt sad that she had never seen the sea and had only been to the river once, when she was ten, when her father took her there in secret and told her how their ancestors had lived there on the banks of the river for thousands of years. The surrounding areas had been damaged decades ago and turned into ruins during the civil disturbances and subsequent divisions between the new conurbation and the borderlands of the ruins, where people had chosen some pretty harsh habitats, overgrown with trees, to make it easier for them to hide when necessary.

She asked herself: could the river be near to this place, where Shihab had brought her one dark night. Or possibly a lake that she hadn't heard of before? She was about to put the question to him when she stopped herself noticing how strangely he was looking at her. She looked at him in turn and a tense silence ensued between them.

'Why would someone kill someone else, Dhai?'

She answered his question with another question: 'Because of evil or greed?' to which he replied, 'Only that?'

He didn't wait for her answer, and a mocking smile came over his lips.

He came nearer to her, so she moved back until she pressed against the wooden wall. Instinctively, she realised that the person in front of her was not the same one she had known for the last year or so. His body language, his looks and the tone of his voice told her she was facing an enemy, not an ally, so she wasn't surprised when his blows and kicks followed one after the other; her only surprise was the intensity of the pain, which was like no other she had experienced before.

As he pulled her towards the bed, she could neither resist nor move. She felt she had lost the power to feel anything. She became a senseless, lifeless entity. She shut her eyes and brought back to mind the sight of the kingfisher, imagining scenarios in which she would follow it from one land to another.

–7–

Shihab had been driving around the city streets since morning, thinking endlessly about the look on the murdered woman's face in her final moments, and turning over in his mind how the case will be presented to the public, and seen from every angle. He didn't care to think too deeply about anything except when he was driving through the streets. He couldn't stand sitting in his office, even though it was spacious and light, completely different from the cramped, dimly-lit designs of ordinary citizens' homes and workplaces. As he drove, he tried not to notice the gigantic buildings and towers so that they didn't affect his mood, knowing better than anyone their overall belittling and taming effect.

Memories of his last visit to the 'land of the savages' the previous year assailed him. The smells of burning and charring invaded him, as did the sight of tents and huts being levelled before being set on fire. He was standing on a nearby hill, watching his men carry out his orders, knowing full well that other identical teams were right now carrying out the same orders on other gatherings of savages stationed in the ruins of the old city that had gone to seed so many decades ago. He recalled the smouldering ruins, saturated with the smell of fire and clouded in smoke, and his appreciation of order and civilisation increased, as he drove from his mind the longing that he felt, from time to time, to liberate himself and escape. He regretted his moment of impulse with Dhai. He realised he should never have involved himself with someone of savage pedigree.

'It's time for this adventure to end and its effects to be wiped out.'

He laughed when he thought about this sentence, because his relationship with Dhai had been woven from the beginning from the threads of endings. He reminded himself that only those who set the rules and those charged with maintaining them were allowed to evade them. For example, gatherings were legally forbidden in the New Age. Even cafés and restaurants were not allowed more than five tables, but any number of leaders and theorists could gather in private meetings and closed circles, so long as they remained secret.

He pushed the scenes of destruction out of his mind and tried to think of something else. But so much thick smoke stayed clinging to his mind that it clouded his vision and muddied the boundaries of the reality in front of him. He put this down to his recent insomnia; he had barely been able to sleep of late, except for short periods, after which he would wake with a violent headache. The previous night, in particular, he hadn't slept at all. He had left Dhai's hut at daybreak to go back to the conurbation, since when he had been going round and round trying to put his thoughts in order. Until now, he'd never known what was going on in her head or what she thought of him or felt about him. This hadn't bothered him much, but deep down he sometimes wondered about it. What happened between them last night left no room for doubt, however. He was haunted by her wounded, tearful eyes and could not get them out of his thoughts. He reckoned that his failure was a result of being affected by her pride as she tried in vain to hide her sobs and to remain calm. Maybe if she had shouted and pleaded with him, he would not have been haunted by the image of her like this.

He thought about the shopping centre mad woman's final moments, as she dug her nails into her killer's arms, and about the blood dripping then congealing on the bedcover and floor, and told himself some deeds might seem evil on the surface but could be good and even noble in their essence. The distinction lay in what was hoped to be achieved through them and the evil and chaos they might prevent in the longer term. It occurred to him that the dividing line between civilisation and savagery was a fine one, and that the preceding decades had proven that history did not always go forwards as some might suppose but rather, in the space of a few months, could equally take us backwards, several decades. All across the world, today, progress jostles and juxtaposes with barbarism, the future with the distant past. In some nations, civilisation had swallowed up savagery, but in most of them the opposite had happened. He would never allow that to be repeated here, so long as he could prevent it.

He recalled the mosquito-blown marshes, the unpaved roads, and the sheer lack of infrastructure in the ruins and imagined this spreading into every inch of his world; the thought seized him with terror. Even if someone were to argue that the present regime was the cause of misery for people in those regions and benefited directly from keeping them in this state, for almost a hundred years, he would not have been persuaded that there was anything wrong in that. For the civil strife that had broken out years ago had initially threatened to destroy absolutely everything and there had been no choice but to dislodge the rebels and drive them out of the new conurbation. Over time, the first founders realised the existence of these people acted as kind of 'scarecrow', helpful for preserving security. They frightened the new city's inhabitants into thinking any disturbance to the regime would lead to their conurbation becoming like the wastelands themselves – a place of darkness and chaos, where disease and epidemics ran wild. But however beneficial they had once been, as a deterrent, about a year ago he ordered their banishment when it became clear they were more of a threat than anything else. He knew better than anyone the temptation they were beginning to represent in the minds of more romantic citizens. He had already recorded the numbers of those who had slipped into the ruins to join them, preferring savagery and the absence of rules to civilisation and laws. His role now was to track down the survivors of the last attack and to block the way for any future escapees.

He remembered the sight of The Professor curled up and trembling in a corner after seeing the murdered woman's face displayed on the screens in the central wilderness facility, and he felt an intoxicating sense of victory. As he sat watching this scene, over and over, he came to the conclusion his former colleague had lost some of his intellectual acuity. He made no effort to hide the way he felt, knowing better than anyone that his every move was being monitored. To his credit, he at least realised that this projection of the aftermath of the 'accident' was primarily for his benefit. Shihab wished there was a way for him to penetrate The Professor's mind to read his thoughts and feelings as soon as they occurred, even though, admittedly, there was a special pleasure in deducing and predicting things. He longed for those times when he and The Professor would compete with each other silently. Perhaps if he had postponed overthrowing him a little while longer, he would not be so bored now. It saddened him that even the most brilliant minds do not entirely escape fatal stupidity in some areas. Otherwise, how could the person with the skill and learning of the founder of the wilderness facilities not realise that this seemingly smooth method of punishment hides within it a complex network of oppression, complicity and concealment?

He pushed away the thought of The Professor, and Dhai's face mixed together with the face of the shopping centre madwoman in his head. The smell of fire came back to him, and his soul was filled with a smoke that could not be drained or diluted. He drove his car towards his house, intending to take a sleeping pill that would give him a few more hours of forced sleep.

-8-

Wounded, bloodied, her body covered with bruises and sores, Dhai left the hut, dragging her legs with difficulty. She knew that Shihab was betting on her not daring to save herself, and it was this precisely that fed her desire to flee and sharpened her will to be free. She didn't think about her fate; she knew he would be able to find her no matter how far away she went, but despite that, she gambled on trying to escape. If she didn't try, she would despise herself even more than she already did now. What would distinguish her from an animal, if she gave in to this pattern of life with him, especially knowing that he didn't intend to ever take her with him to the conurbation. He could never forget that she grew up in the ruins and was descended from rebels. As she trudged painfully through the tangled trees, the image of the cheerful bird with its turquoise back and bright orange breast came to mind. She felt grateful for this beautiful creature, because its very existence in this world made her feel at peace.

Besides the kingfisher, an improvised map of the area was imprinted on her mind, at the centre of which lay a lake or river, which comforted her in a vague way. She decided that this would be her desired destination, just as those circular clearings in the middle of the woods had been the places her family, and those she had grown up with, had gravitated to. They used to call them 'Mayadeen'[1] and they made their way to them on specific dates to stand there humbly, reciting specific sentences and chants. Her father had told her one day that a generation of ancestors had prepared these empty spaces, between the trees, after they settled in the wilderness in remembrance of their past and to protest against the patterns of urban planning the New Age had adopted in the conurbation, against which they themselves had rebelled. They had chosen to hide in the forests to protect themselves and their children from possible attacks from the forces of the New Age. Successive generations inherited their care for these 'mayadeen' as places of refuge.

On her way to the body of water – which she didn't realise was a river extending from great equatorial lakes in the south, and flowed into a vast sea in the north – Dhai stumbled on the severed trunk of a tree squatting among the other trees. She screamed from the pain and fell to the ground, whereupon she was surprised by a man, untidy in appearance with a sprouting beard, who came up to help her. She told him she wanted to get to the water where the kingfisher was to be found. He looked at her in confusion and made no comment. As he helped her get to her feet, his experienced eyes did not fail to notice her bruises. She examined him in turn and concluded that his unkempt appearance was something new to him. She deduced this from his carefully trimmed nails and the softness of his hands compared to the neglected appearance of those who lived out here.

She walked beside him, and he slowed down so as not to get too far in front of her. Whenever she tired, he supported her. She was afraid to irritate him by chattering, in case he might leave her alone in this maze of trees, but he, on the other hand, bombarded her with questions: Where had she come from? What had caused these injuries and bruises? Where did she think she was going? His stern manner reminded her of Shihab, so she turned her face away as if to push the latter's memory away from her.

She learned from him that the scattered communities living among the ruins had been finally cleared out and their remains burned about a year ago. She thought about this length of time and calculated that it had happened immediately after Shihab had moved her to her new spot. She asked about the residents, or rather, those who had escaped the epidemic that had killed her parents and most of her friends, and he told her that most of them had been killed, so far as he knew. He didn't add much to what she already understood from what she had heard in the past about previous raids in the region.

-9-

Shihab woke from a sleep that was so deep it was almost a

coma. For a few seconds, his identity, his past, and all his knowledge were lost to him, which gave him a peaceful feeling he seldom experienced. Then he woke to his life as he knew it and felt depressed despite himself. He checked his screen to update himself on his team's messages one by one, then put the screen aside and got up to shower. The smell of burning was still nesting inside him when he emerged from the shower and sat down to eat his breakfast, looking at the city through the wide window facing his dining table. He wondered: Should he give Dhai some time or should he surprise her right away? Again, her face merged in his mind with the face of the dead woman. As he put on his outdoor clothes, and got ready for another drive, he noticed scratch marks, running the length of his right arm, and examined them indifferently.

Minutes later, he was in his car – his favourite place in this world – but before setting off, he picked up his screen and sent clear and specific messages to his team. He barely looked ahead as he drove. His mind wandered to all sorts of faraway places, and he felt more immune than ever. Immediately, The Professor came into his thoughts, and he laughed uncontrollably, as he said to himself: 'Not this sort of immunity; my immunity is real, no doubt about it!'

–10–

The river was nothing like how Dhai remembered it. She thought its waters had receded and that more grass and sedge surrounded it than before. She heard the clucking of birds and the chirping of grey and brown sparrows, but she found no trace of the kingfisher and thought that this was a bad omen. She was sure Shihab would find her anyway, or perhaps he wanted her to flee for some purpose of his own, otherwise why hadn't he locked the hut door on her or chained her up inside it? This couldn't be just because he trusted she wouldn't dare try to escape, not after what happened between them the night before.

THE WILDERNESS FACILITIES

Her companion was tense, looking around him all the time. He sat on a nearby rock, while she lay on the grass next to it, her eyes fixed on the shrunken area of water surrounded by sedge and native reeds. She suddenly asked him if he knew Shihab. The question seemed stupid the moment she asked it. Just because they were both from the conurbation didn't mean they knew each other. But his agitation the moment he heard the question made her think that her enquiry had not been as stupid as she had imagined a moment before.

'Where do you know him from?'

He became a hostile person all of a sudden, as if his previous kindness was just a shell he had quickly shed.

'He arrested my brother...' she added.

'And ordered the wastelands to be burned and cleared of their residents.'

Dhai didn't reply, for an armed unit had suddenly raided the place, and anyway she had no reply to give. Her brain stopped working and her words dried up. They beat her companion black and blue, but they didn't resort to violence with her. In the end, they led them both to an armoured vehicle, which took them to the city for interrogation about a murder, or so Dhai understood from the few words exchanged between the members of the unit. Before the vehicle moved off, Dhai took one last look at the river but the kingfisher was nowhere to be seen.

-11-

Dhai appeared on the display screens with a face marked by bruises whose colour varied between violet and blue. Nothing gave away its previous beauty, except for her wide eyes, now full of fear. In an exhausted voice, she told how she had slipped into the city from the ruins and succeeded in avoiding the surveillance cameras with the help of the official from the main surveillance centre, whom she had met through her brother, who was presently detained in one of the wilderness facilities. At this point, there appeared beside her on the screen a man with a sprouting beard and unkempt hair. The camera quickly moved away from him and focused on the young woman, as she added that if she had not met him, she would not have known where to go in this maze of extraordinarily large buildings and parallel and intersecting streets, as she came from the ruins. She described at length how, as she was walking alone on the street, she noticed the victim also walking alone at an intersection, and had followed her and entered the building after her. She said the woman seemed confused and in a different world, which made it easy for her to hide in the entrance to the building, then contrive to enter her flat at night. She didn't clarify how she had done this; she merely stated in a shaky voice that her aim was to persuade her victim to let her stay with her until she had arranged her affairs, but the woman, who had been surprised by someone breaking into her bedroom, took fright and started to scream, so there was no alternative but to silence her at any cost.

Dhai's confessions were followed by a voice-over in which it emerged that more detailed investigations had established conclusive proof that the matter was actually more complicated than this, and that there was an organisation led by an internal fifth column which included among its members a group of thugs from the ruins, whose objective was to destabilise the regime and spread the chaos of the 'savage lands' everywhere. The official spokesman made a promise to the honourable citizens to discover the names of the traitors and detain them in wilderness facilities very soon.

Shihab sat in his office, his eyes glued to a screen as wide as the entire wall, his mind devoid of any thought whatsoever.

Note

1. Mayadeen; squares.

Drowning

Heba Khamis

Translated by Maisa Almanasreh

Alexandria

FROM UNDER THE COLD marble threshold of the Grand Mosque, insects swarmed.[1] Like a mountain spring, they surged in their multitudes, flowing at full tilt from beneath the building's marble doorstep, as though escaping a dread that lurked beneath, heading up and away from the sea, which was expected to flood any day now.

Beneath that cold marble threshold, where blood was once spilled, beneath the city's concrete walls and salty waters, a beast dwelt. Every year it would release the insects to alert us to its awakening and remind us it was time to hide. For many years, it had plagued the city, always emerging from its hiding place at high tide, prophesying doom. All cities have a history they cannot escape from, and the beast was part of ours.

It had just started to rain, but it was a light drizzle, still bearable compared to what awaited us in the coming months once we went into hiding. Every year, at the end of October, we would start to come together to stockpile supplies. Enough to cover the duration of our retreat up into the high-rises, when the sea-water would swell into our city's streets, and the beast that lived below the city would rise up, bringing with him the spirits of all those who departed around a century ago. For years, life in the city had been following its normal course, until the arrival of these salty waters marked the departure of so many spirits, staining the seawater a dark colour as it flooded into the city's streets; streets that became deserted around this time of the year.

On the steps of the Grand Mosque, with its fresh sea air, I managed to catch my breath. I had just run away from my parents' house to chase my dream alongside the rest of the masses. In my head, I pictured my dream coming true. This gave me the comfort I needed beyond the warmth of the scratchy wool blanket that I wrapped around myself, inside one of the tents in the square by the Grand Mosque.

Around me, the chants had begun to gradually fade. Most of the young crowd was preparing to go to sleep and mark an end to this long Friday, a day that had seen them triumph over the black-uniformed men and their armoured vehicles. They shook off their clothes and tents to remove the smell of tear gas, and tales of love and the future rose into the air.

It was in this crowd that I first picked out the quiet boy, constantly wiping his glasses to clear them of the tears brought on by the gas. While it was too dark to make out the colour of his thin shirt, watching him tremble gave me the shivers. A girl noticed me shaking and offered me some bread and cheese, inviting me to share her meal. She was part of a group who appeared almost identical, all covering their faces. Some used a niqab, while others wore the Palestinian kufiyah.

'They grabbed me by my niqab, may God punish them,' one of them said. 'If it weren't for the veil that my comrades had given me, I wouldn't have managed to cover my face and protect myself from the tear gas.'

DROWNING

Another group of comrades, many with injuries to their legs, approached us as on their way towards the Al-Amiri Hospital next to the mosque. They examined the injured among us and then they left. Meanwhile, I couldn't take my eyes off that boy in the dark shirt. Unlike the rest of us, he had not asked for a blanket to keep him warm, and instead left his body to shiver from the sweat and the cold.

Over the past few days, I had watched the street from my window at home, looking onto Almansheyeh Square and the empty base of the Muhammad Ali statue, now long gone. After my grandmother passed away, my parents had moved into her old apartment. From inside my small, high-ceilinged bedroom at grandmother's old house, that window was the source of all my learning. During my teenage years, I gazed out over the run-down hotels overlooking the square and listened to the prostitutes whose giggles I could hear behind the damp windows at night. And in the morning, I woke up to the smell of sugar wafting up from the candy factories on the ground floors of the neighbouring buildings.

As an only child, being stuck indoors with my parents all day made me the centre of attention, not as a spoiled daughter, but as a mural on which all my parents' disappointments were commemorated. When the walls of the old house started to crack, my mother reprimanded me, but she would never blame my father for not submitting to the rules of the revolutionary movement like all the others. She had decided to remain married to him even though she knew she deserved better, so she dumped all her resentment on me. As for my father, he would curse the day he bore a daughter, especially every time he was reminded of his inability to fix even the simplest of things, like mending a broken toilet seat or repairing the damp house walls. For him, having a daughter was like holding onto a bedroom chair on which all the useless items that found no other place in the house piled up. I was an object whose value no one acknowledged, despite its evident functionality, and every time the clutter was cleared from it, it would be considered dispensable again, yet nobody would actually dare throw it away.

On the first day of the chants, I watched the protestors emerge from the narrow alleys to congregate at the centre of the big square by the seaside. The square was like a heart, drawing fresh blood through the vein-like streets into it. I watched the crowds break through walls of lined-up soldiers and form into a large mass in the square, only for the soldiers to attack them again, a few hours later, chasing them back into the alleyways around the square.

On the first Friday following that, I devised my plan to leave my parents' home to go out on the streets. I followed all the instructions, leaving my mobile phone behind after setting it to silent and disconnecting it from all networks. I walked through the side streets into the alleyways, carefully avoiding the scattered clusters of soldiers. When I arrived at the quiet St. Catherine's Cathedral, I turned towards the spice alleys, looking for any crowd I could join. I heard the voices coming from afar and started to tremble.

Feeling lonely exposes your vulnerability and leaves you more fragile. As I stood there alone on the street by the seafront, I had to challenge my own thoughts to calm myself down. I found myself standing there and watching, as though none of this were happening. I felt afraid to engage but I knew I had to, so I kept following the tramlines, surprised by the pungent smell that increased as I approached the Grand Mosque by the seafront.

The wailing of sirens served as an appropriate background for the scene. As the noise faded into the distance, the masses marching towards the mosque grew bigger, so I followed their lead and kept close to them, strongly believing the spirit of unity that hovered over our heads was sheltering us from harm. None of us had noticed the guns at this stage, we were too busy celebrating our victory, having driven the soldiers back in fear.

DROWNING

As night fell, our cadre of young comrades divided into groups to take shifts standing guard, and the boy in the dark shirt stayed with them. Many of them stared at their phones, vigilantly waiting for reassurance or trying to regain communications with the rest of the group. But the phone networks were down. After most had fallen asleep, I stayed up watching the boy. Someone had given him a scarf to cover his body against the cold. After dozing off just for a moment, I was startled awake by the sudden sound of gunfire. I pulled the wool blanket over my head, trembling at the thought of bullets whizzing by. In that moment, I was terrified by the closeness of death. I yearned for my small bedroom, and I longed for my parents and the old rundown house, realising how utterly far away all this seemed right now. I raised my head up only to see the boy in the dark shirt sitting still in his scarf; he was completely motionless, until he moved his bare head ever so slightly in my direction.

At that moment, a bullet came whistling from the top of a nearby building, piercing straight into the boy's head. His eyes remained wide open, gazing at me. The blood that spilled onto the asphalt and along the marble steps of the mosque trickled downwards, beneath us, disappearing into the ground. The boy lay there lifeless with his head perforated, slumping onto the tram's iron track. Moments later, the streak of blood had completely vanished. I heard the boy whispering in my ear, as if I was being spoken to by his cold, dead body: he whispered remnants of chants, then told me I would die next, and asked if I would stay completely still, so that I too could follow him into the ground.

I was horrified by this voice lingering in the air, with his body just lying there in front of me. So, I moved a few steps away, dodging the unseen bullet that pierced the tent fabric and the woollen blanket. The girl beside me woke up in a panic, frantically checking her body for traces of the bullet. I don't remember what happened in the moments after. All I recall is the sound of the gravel under my feet as I ran along the tram tracks as far as the station, taking shelter there from the stray bullets for the next few hours until sunrise.

At the front door to the house, they received me in silence. I headed straight to my bedroom, a place that just a little while back had seemed to me like a long-lost paradise. The voice continued to echo in my ear, but deeper this time, as if filling the air to form a phantom of the boy who had lain in front of me so lifelessly what felt like moments before. I froze before him, while he kept repeating his last movement, his head bare, murmuring the rest of the chant. Suddenly he approached me and whispered in my ear 'You will live for many years to witness the drowning of the city, and my return.'

The rhythm of his voice was strong and steady, like a hum. And as soon as he finished his sentence, he completely disappeared, although the chants continued to echo in my ear.

*

For years, they continued to bury the city, building over green spaces and blocking any view of the sea with their skyscrapers. New developments crept into the sea, and along the edges of the lake, on the other side of the city, they created man-made hills and built high-walled castles. From up there, they could watch everything taking place in the city that now resembled a sinkhole, flanked by the sea on one side and the still lake on the other.

Then, one winter day, the sea raged, rising into a rebellion that did not subside like ours had done. For decades, I had dreamt of going back to that day in the marble square in front of the mosque. I had spent a long life hoping to meet the destiny that had awaited me on that day. But that chance had passed, instead I spent years searching in other people's faces for the boy, whose whispers still echoed in my ear. Every winter, on the anniversary of that Friday, I sat on the cold doorstep of the mosque, waiting for the bullet that had eluded me all those years ago. On one of these occasions, I witnessed the sea revolt with my own eyes, its waves rising so high, submerging the lower streets of the city. Sitting there, I drew up my cold feet so the water would not reach them, and watched people's faces, in the street, as they jumped up onto higher ground so as not to get wet.

A few years later, the sea became a regular winter guest of the city, flooding its streets, and driving the owners of the high-rises inland, where they kept to their closed communities and watched from afar. The lower floors of these high-rises were abandoned by their inhabitants, and their foundations left to be corroded by the sea more and more each day.

Even after the sea flooded the streets, it was still possible to live in the city. We found ways to circumvent the water and adapt our lives around it. The residents of the lower floors abandoned their apartments, and the run-down houses in the poorer neighbourhoods crumbled into the sea. While the sea corroded the foundations of the buildings and stripped the houses of their stones, the residents of the lower floors sought shelter with those living in higher ones. In some neighbourhoods, the owners of the faraway mansions came back to tour the flooded city streets with their boats, making the most of the abundance of water and enjoying new leisure activities. None of them noticed the house doors that were drowning under water or the residents that were trapped inside their homes and forced to escape through narrow windows.

*

The situation might have continued this way for years. We could have gotten used to navigating the water and figuring out the most convenient way to leave a house through its windows whenever the water got too high, but the sea stirred up something that had lived in the depths for decades. At first, those living near the mosque on the seafront complained about hearing screams at night, but no one believed them. But when the seawater turned the colour of blood, we wished we could disbelieve our own eyes, but we couldn't.

In my life I have carried countless babies in my womb that never went full term, sending them all back to mother earth in the hope that, if I nurtured her, she would grant me one child that would grow to completion inside me, one that I would give birth to. But she refused. For many years, I nourished the marble doorstep of the mosque with my prayers, trying to escape from something trapped inside me, unaware of what it was. I chased a phantom that would never appear to me. I began to age but I did not die. I lived my entire life without ever getting sick or perishing like everyone else I knew. My skin grew pale, with hard bones beneath, my face was full of wrinkles and my long hair white like snow. I leant on a cane, old like me, never moving more than a few yards from my home on the square by the sea, next to the mosque.

*

A hundred years have now passed since that Friday when I almost died. The city has aged and deteriorated just like me. And every winter, the sea comes back to flood its streets. In the days following a flood, the insects emerge from cracks in the ground to warn us that the beast is about to rise, before the water turns blood red. I alone notice these signs of its imminent appearance and dare to walk near its territory. Each time, I would place a few Qurans on the steps of the mosque, hoping this might save us from the coming evil, then roam the nearby streets loudly warning people, so they can stockpile their food and stay safe in their homes.

No one saw the beast roaming the city's streets, but we all heard him, and saw the spirits trapped below furiously stirring the water around them to form a stream that went all the way from the mosque to the square, like a parade. The path where blood had once been spilt could still remember those who died upon it, feeding the earth beneath with their blood. We heard stories about all the lifeless bodies that the beast left behind. We tried to make our voices heard by those from the suburbs, but they sailed around us with their boats in the blood-tinted waters with nothing to say. None of them heard the shouts that preceded the beast's rising, nor felt the cold breeze that chilled our blood. We were silently drowning in our agony, without knowing why the beast was punishing us.

*

On marble threshold of the great mosque, whilst the insects surged towards the tram rails, I found serenity. From below those steps, the beast appeared to me fully in the form of the boy with the perforated head, his eyes calm and his hair wild, trembling from the cold in his dark shirt.

He came closer to me, and I heard his soft voice dancing in my ear:

'You died once before on these steps, your first death.'

Abruptly I found myself returning to that tragic Friday. I reached up to touch my head and discovered my forehead was also perforated. Only in that moment did I come to realise that I was the one who had tinted the seawater that flooded our city's streets with the colour of blood.

Note

1. The mosque referred to in this story is the Al-Qaed Ibrahim Mosque, or the Commander Ibrahim Mosque, which saw a significant gathering of protestors during the 2011 Revolution. On Friday 28 January, 2011, it witnessed a massacre conducted by unidentified snipers targeting civilians, as part of a pattern of massacres across Egypt on that day, designed to instill panic. These massacres have never been properly documented, with the few reports that were made at the time being subsequently expunged from Egyptian media archives.

Everything is Great in Rome

Ahmed El-Fakharany

Translated by Robin Moger

-1-

THE MORNING OF JANUARY 25th, 2111 – otherwise known as National Police Day – we woke to find that Tahrir Square was no more and in its place stood the Colosseum, the most magnificent and brutal sporting arena in history. Vast advertising hoardings overran the country: a blonde in a long loose robe pinned at the shoulders with a sash round her waist, and from her mouth, bright colours shimmering skittishly, a slogan singing out – *Everything's Great in Rome* – which was taken up as the cornerstone of a national media campaign.

Daily fights at the Colosseum, so we were given to understand: live broadcast combat. Attendees would be chosen by a national lottery and betting would be open to all.

'The president's gift to his people,' the TV presenters and talking heads kept saying. Though illegal, wrestling in backstreet fighting pits was the nation's favourite sport, and now the presenters were claiming that this might not be his last gift, either; that the Colosseum was, maybe, only a test run of the latest in cutting-edge technology: a technique for grafting onto our capital the genes of another city entirely. In a few short years, Cairo itself could be completely remodelled into classical Rome! The first fully-transfigured city in the world, the realisation of a vision that had first visited the president in the solitude of his sanctuary. And why should it stop there? We might find ourselves in a different city every day: Paris, New Delhi, Dubai, Bogota, Washington, Cape Town…

None of this came as a surprise. The true shock was the announcement that after nearly half a century of prayers and pleas, the president had decided to bring his long confinement to an end and appear before his people. Unconfirmed reports suggested that he would attend the Colosseum's opening show in person.

'I have grown weary. You are no longer children, a lost people hanging its sins and errors around my neck. I set you on the right path, having lifted from you the burden of the most grievous evils. I have been cursed in your place. Today your turn has come and you must finish the task yourselves. I leave you with your responsibilities and without advice. I leave you on your own.'

His tone in this final speech had seemed aloof, reserved, and in his gaze we sensed a profound sadness directed against us in particular. Though his features were pale and drawn, a glowing halo circled his face, and regardless of whether he really had decided to leave us or continue his work as president, it seemed as though he would be gone from us forever.

His absence lasted 50 years. It was said that he was in some secret hideaway, searching for the absolute and eternal truth of good and evil. There was no announcement that he had passed away and no new president was appointed in his place; all that remained of him were the recordings of his speeches up to and including that final one, a perpetual loop that ran on huge screens the length and breadth of the country. To some, the essence of his deep wisdom became clearer over time, gaining through exegesis the stamp of divine instruction, the impact of an intimate whisper, a veiled threat.

Theories circulated, among them that he had benefitted from scientific advances available to only a small minority of the world's elite, and that it was these that had allowed him to conquer the ageing process; like a saint had lived among us without our knowledge. Another theory claimed that what had happened was no more than your standard coup: he'd been forced to read his resignation speech, then had either been executed or had wasted away in some secret prison. It was just that the coup leaders had realised that they could exploit the images broadcast on those screens, that they could rule the country together as partners, invisible and equal, with no man more powerful than the next.

We went on with our lives, our faith in his all-encompassing and active presence outspoken, our faint doubts dormant, unspoken, and punishable by law. At night, of course, we would hear the entreaties offered up by his devotees, those whose love of the president, their sense of his sanctity and hope that he might return to save us from the country's current state of brutality, incompetence and corruption, was only bolstered by his absence. Occasionally, the failure to intervene of 'our lord' (as the true believers called him) would move them to rage.

But over the last decade, as the ruling class began to weaken and fray, as the country sank into poverty, these ripples of doubt became waves and there were redoubled rumours of plots hatched by night to seize the state. Voices began to clamour for more than mere shadows and pictures, for a new flesh-and-blood leader to revive memories of the hidden president and the resolute will of his early days in office, to lift from our necks the burden of error and take it on himself.

Unlike his predecessors, Our Lord had never shammed democracy or a belief in human rights for the West; he was crystal clear when it came to what he had in store for the country: an iron fist with no pretence at a reprieve, save a promise he made to the poor, that his unsparing economic measures would ultimately be in their interests. He made no attempt to justify or gloss over his approach and, his grip on power now established and with a frank and undisguised violence, he brought to an end the freedoms we'd won at the end of the previous president's term. Abolishing all forms of elections he abrogated the constitution and without a second thought, isolated the country from the rest of the world. Warrants of execution were signed as offhandedly as you might wish a man good morning, then carried out in the public squares.

After two decades of absolute rule – at least, as some would later read into his final speech – the president realised the magnitude of his error: his heart told him that he had been led into the trap of sacrificing himself for us. His decision to withdraw into seclusion was preceded by the intimations of an incipient mysticism, cryptic phrases scattered through his speeches that betrayed a torment eating at their speaker's soul. Though we did not pick up on the signs at the time.

Devotees rejoiced at the news of his imminent appearance (in response to their wishes and counter to his own), while the uncharitable said that the reports proved he, like all those who taste power, was unable to relinquish it; fearful of losing his grip, he had no other choice. He had even decided to assert his presence in the most conventional of ways, the hallowed tradition of emperors everywhere: inaugurating a building.

-2-

The roar, choking the throats of the crowd. 'Hercules!' they chant, 'Hercules!'

They mean Abdel Moula. His dark, sweating, chiselled body, a veritable god of homicide, is down in the ring-fenced round by the cage of death, the whole structure hidden away in a back alley both far from the eyes of the government and right beneath its feet.

'Where did they find this miracle?' asks one man, and another replies, 'An enchanted city in the sands of Mauritania, where the savages are as gaudy and carefully hidden as wildflowers in hell…'

The truth is that Abdel Moula is a peasant from a remote and indigent village in the south, though he makes no effort to repudiate any of the myths that are circulated about him. He even lets his supporters calls him Hercules. His fame, eclipsing the truth of his origins, weaves a thousand stories round him.

He has killed everyone who's ever joined him in the ring, warrior after warrior, adventurer after adventurer, brute by brute, in secret prizefights whose existence is known to all and denied by all, informal contests with only the single rule: that each end with a victor still breathing and a second man dead.

The spectators toss weapons through openings in the cage: wooden bats, swords, sickles, iron bars, chopping knives, skinning knives, cleavers. Not to Abdel Moula, though. Only to his opponent, to make it more interesting. Abdel Moula doesn't use weapons, never touches them, though blood's claws be breaking through his skin. His opponents might be twice his size, but their eyes do not roar with life (or, incongruously, with freedom) as Abdel Moula's do.

Outside the cage of death, Abdel Moula is quiescent; reverting to a dead-eyed, biddable drudge. His mouth framing only inaudible mutterings, he looks at no man; indeed, he rolls his eyes inward, blank and terrifying, licks his clotting, murderous wounds, and trembles with fear. But in minutes, the cuts are healed as though they never were. A miracle that no one can account for. A body enchanted.

The shouting swells. This is the crowd's favourite part, when the victim is anointed with something more precious than death. No one knows which victim will be chosen: the eighth, the tenth, the first? He might not do it at all. Abdel Moula, an idiot outside the ring, knows exactly what he is doing in it, and for this they love him. He has made himself a star; has devised for himself a prize quite other than that of his life or the food on his family's table. They have made action figures of him, have printed his portrait on cheap T-shirts, have released songs in his praise; even the higher echelons of government secretly bet on his fights though they'd never acknowledge his fame.

The chosen victim submits absolutely to the fate that Abdel Moula places in the hands of his supporters. All they have to do is turn their thumbs down.

They do not disappoint. With his bare fingers, Hercules splits open the chest of his victim, who by now has ceased all movement, his pleas for mercy reduced to an expression of dull acceptance. Extracting the heart, he takes a bite from it, spits it out, then hoists the remnant high into the frenzy and din of the crowd. For a few seconds he holds it there, victorious, then comes the moment when he gazes out at the crowd with joy and scorn, like a man who has taken life's wonder in his grasp only to see it slip away through his fingers.

There might be others fighting before him or once he's done, but Hercules is the pearl that sets the big bets in motion, that sends sales of food and drugs and alcohol rocketing sky-high.

But today is different to all the others in his life. Today, as soon as the show is over, the police raid the ring.

Despite their unspoken agreement with the government, the organisers of these informal fights are used to police raids, which are only ever designed to extort them and corner a share of the profits. This time, however, the police want only one thing, to detain Abdel Moula, who submits without resistance as they handcuff and blindfold him, then lead him to the back of a truck.

-3-

The guards uttered not a word the whole way, just smoked in murderous silence. Abdel Moula didn't have to be a genius to realise that they had left Cairo behind, the jarring, dead roar of the city fading away and rising up in its place the sounds inside his soul: echoes of frog croaks, ghouls' wounded roars, creaking mills, the muffled screams of homeless children in the throats of the demons swallowing them and, worst of all, the moans of his victims.

Outside the ring, he was perpetually dogged by the terrified, pleading expressions that he encountered in the faces of opponents as he took their lives. It was a secret he held deep inside, and one that threatened to bring him down. If exposed, his aura would break and his livelihood be lost; from merciless killing machine to frightened child. He had a family hanging round his neck and he couldn't give them up to starvation. His wages barely kept hunger at bay as it was, while an endless chain of bookkeepers and promoters were kept wealthy in his wake.

He felt the truck climb rocky slopes then level out over smooth ground.

His exhaustion, coupled first with the steady rhythm of the truck's growl then the cries of the ghouls and ghosts inside him, had sent him into a doze from which he was woken by the hiss of rain and the angry roar of the wind being forced through tight spaces. Then silence fell again, and as this silence gave way to a tremendous pounding – loud as thunder, loud as the end of the world – the truck came to a halt. The guards shoved him out and his body immediately began to shake from the bitter cold. He had to clench hard to stopper his exploding bladder. They untied the blindfold without freeing his hands and allowed him to piss where he stood. He was on an empty desert plain. A thick grey mist was all about him, as though wrung out from the sky.

Then they walked, and when they emerged from the mist saw a great citadel rising from the plain, and crowning it a soaring tower that seemed to brush the clouds. The citadel appeared impregnable, surmounting a tangle of rough mountain tracks.

He climbed, driven by their clubs, till they came to a narrow pathway leading up to the citadel's main gate. Slowly it opened, and out clopped a high-ranking officer followed by a troupe of masked men on camel-back, whips in their hands and guns slung across their backs.

The officer was in his fifties, of medium height, eagles on his epaulettes. With a Mameluke turban wound round his head, he wore a sword at his waist, and Abdel Moula recognised him immediately: Mourad Bey, Commander of the Cairo Guard. The chief of police, in other words. The change of title had been an early instance of Our Lord's inexplicable whims.

Bestowing on him a gracious smile, Mourad Bey apologised for 'an entirely unintentional error' and chastised the head of the guards who had dragged him here so unceremoniously. He ordered that the handcuffs be removed then permitted the guards to take a picture with their hero.

When they were done, he took Abdel Moula's arm like an old friend and led him inside, into a vast and surpassingly beautiful garden of rare plants ringed by cages that held lions and snakes and endangered animals of every kind. The citadel was laid on the Mameluke pattern. To the east was the haremlik – the women's quarters – and looking round he saw more: lodgings for slaves and serving boys, the stables, feast halls for the soldiers. There were extraordinary fountains that seemed to redefine the physics of what water could do, perpetually washing the air clean.

They came to the keep's great gate. Abdel Moula gaped like a child at the two statues that guarded it. The statues had human faces and lions' feet, wings like eagles and the bodies of bulls. He had seen their like before in his dreams but had never known how to interpret them: were they summoning him to some supernatural transformation, or were they sentinels, somehow barring his way forward, even in a dream?

'Where am I?' he said,

'In the president's palace,' answered Mourad Bey.

And flushed by passion, Abdel Moula breathed, 'Our Lord…' Without intending it, his gaze swept up the tower. It was as though two huge eyes were watching him, as though they had been watching him his whole life long, and for all that he was certain, somehow, that his lord sat up there, he could see only shadows and shades, shapes that could have been anything or nothing. He ducked his head.

'This tower,' Mourad Bey was saying, 'revolves to face the sun on a moving base. Who sits up there can see everything.'

They climbed the white marble steps that led to the keep's gate. On one of the steps stood the statue of a Roman soldier brandishing a sword, a severed head beneath his sandal. Three steps on was another soldier leaning on one hand, his other raised. He was headless, and Abdel Moula supposed that he must be the victim of the first.

The balconies on the walls were supported by brackets in the shape of Indian elephants and its windows were mirrored so those inside could look out without being seen.

Mourad Bey led him into a main hall crammed with treasures in gold and platinum. An antique clock gave out the time in minutes and hours, in days and months and years. It showed the phases of the moon and the temperature. There was nothing else like it outside of Buckingham Palace, which now, decades after the end of the British monarchy, was no more than a museum.

Statues of Buddhas and dragons studded the marble and alabaster floor, and the banisters were panelled with bronze sheets and covered in tiny, intricately carved Indian reliefs. The entire palace was so designed that its rooms and hallways would never lose the sun, its walls were hung with works by the great masters, and in every corner stood a statue of an Indian god.

Abdel Moula had seen palaces before, those times he'd been asked to put on private shows for the rich: great homes both more contemporary in design and more dazzling. Some of them could only be described as marvels, things that should only exist in the future or science-fiction. When it came to this building, however, he felt that every step took him deeper and deeper into the distant past. It lacked only a thick carpeting of cobwebs to be a haunted castle.

As he passed a painting on which was written in a bold Kufic script *There is no birth but through death* he stopped. He was peering at it, when Mourad Bey broke in:

'Do you believe in the existence of the president?'

'As much as in mine, or yours,' he answered, startled.

'Good. This country's in need of citizens with a faith like yours.'

Abdel Moula's face suffused with pride.

'A few days from now,' Mourad Bey went on, 'Our Lord himself will open the first day of spectacles at the Colosseum, and he has chosen you to be a part in this unique event, knowing the affection in which the people hold you. This would be the first time you have been officially recognised: you have gone unsung too long.'

'An honour…'

'The show will be exactly what you do every day of the week. A death match. No mercy to the loser.'

Abdel Moula smiled – proud, abashed – and an admiring Mourad Bey took in the white glow of his teeth, then gestured for him to sit. A servant brought drinks and grand platters piled with meats and treats and fruits, and being ravenous he devoured everything set before him. He'd never tasted such delicious fare in his life. Like it was heaven sent.

Mourad Bey watched him eat in silence and, when he was finished, ordered the finest hashish and opium to be brought, and with Abdel Moula stoned and settled, he again signalled to his soldiers, who opened the doors and in trooped dozens of beautiful women from every corner of the earth, of every hue. Abdel Moula had never seen such beauty. They gathered round him and began to lick every inch of his body, and he moaned and moaned as though driving the stink of poverty and the humiliations of his life from his very bones.

'They're all for me?'

Thus Abdel Moula, all innocence; innocent, too, of the look of contempt that crossed Mourad Bey's face.

-4-

He woke to find himself manacled inside a steel cage in a half-lit cell. It stank. He remembered his children and his wife, and felt guilty at the way he had abandoned himself to pleasure the night before without giving them a thought. Then a wave of anxiety swept over him: what was to become of him? Of them? He'd always heard stories about people who had vanished without explanation, who disappeared behind the sun, as the saying had it. Now he had agreed to take part in Our Lord's celebrations, so why had they given him one night of bliss then taken it away? Was he being punished for accepting the food and drugs and women? Had he failed his lord's test? But what would Our Lord know, floating around in the clouds, about the long-denied appetites of his poorest subjects?

Hours passed, and Mourad Bey appeared. He sat in a chair facing the cage, lit a cigarette, then slowly dribbled the smoke out, silently sizing up the savage, imprisoned like a broken beast in his cage.

At last he said, 'You're a hell of fighter, Abdel Moula. I used to come in disguise to watch you. Physically, of course, you're talented, but do you know what your best quality is?'

Abdel Moula said nothing.

'It's your teeth. Strong and long. Look like they could take a bite out of the world itself. Extraordinary really. Our teeth are soft, and our bodies are lost to time.'

'Why have I been caged after last night? What did I do wrong?'

'Nothing. Last night was just to sweeten the deal.'

'I'll do anything.'

'When it's time for your performance in the Colosseum, you'll face a few fighters first and beat them all as usual, but your last opponent will be, well, someone in particular.'

'And what do I have to do?'

'You have to lose to him.'

'You mean I have to die?'

'Precisely.'

'Give me one reason why I should do that.'

'A sacrifice for the homeland! We're going through a serious economic crisis and when the news gets out that you'll be fighting, everyone, rich and poor, is going to bet their house on you winning.'

'And the state will be betting that I die?'

'Sooner or later the promoters of the back-alley fights are going to send you to your death. You're worth less winning all the time and when that death comes it'll make nothing at all. I'm offering you the chance to get fair compensation for your skills, and for a glorious cause into the bargain.'

Abdel Moula stared into Mourad Bey's fierce face, at the haughty expression with its overpowering reek of cunning, at the pompous upturned ends of his moustache, and through this facade of arrogance and self-satisfied power he saw the hidden truth of the man's soul: mean and cowardly.

'No.'

He sighed the word, a breeze freighted with all the bitterness of his life.

The commander of the city guard left the cell with an air of cold detachment, switching off the dim lights as he departed, to leave Abdel Moula in oppressive darkness, a man trapped in the belly of a whale.

-5-

He was left without food or water for two days, alone with a terrible silence in which the moans of his victims reached their peak. He curled up in his cage, trembling. As all true believers did, he prayed to Our Lord, but his pleas quickly turned to anger at the leader whose absence had left them all mired in misery.

Abdel Moula was only 29-years-old. He hadn't been around to witness the president's living presence in our midst. But he did know that the one and only promise the president had made in his recorded speeches was that the sacrifices of the poor would not, in the end, be made in vain, and that the endless humiliation of their daily lives would come to a close.

Now, his very life at stake just so he could feed his children, he first cursed and abused him, then wept and pled forgiveness, chanting his name over and over for hours on end until the dinning chatter of his ghosts died away to be replaced by a single voice, a voice he knew like the back of his hand. Our Lord.

The voice never said anything that made sense—just raving, like charms or spells or prayers of protection—but it was enough to bring him peace. Then, as time went on, the clouded words began to sharpen and clear, a divine whisper telling him that he was a good citizen, that he was happy with him, that it was for his family that Abdel Moula struggled and fought, that he bore his sins with courage and so had been forgiven them all. He would be recompensed with an estate that would never fall to ruin, with a home where he would never go hungry or unclothed, and all that separated him from this was a single footstep. All he had to do was take it.

Our Lord asked: 'Are you willing to take that step?'

Somewhere inside Abdel Moula a muffled ecstasy detonated like a distant thunderclap, then dissipated into a cool sense of contentment. From deep in the belly of the whale, he whispered, 'I always have been.'

The door to the cell opened and the lights came on.

The soldiers led him gently to the great hall. Mourad Bey was sprawled on a couch, peeling an apple which he tossed to Abdel Moula. Plucking it out of the air, Abdel Moula devoured it with the hunger of a full three days in his darkened cell.

Mourad Bey said with a smirk, 'How beautiful is faith.'

'I'm only worrying about my wife and the kids.'

'Don't. They're in the care of our master. He will look after them for life: they'll be moved to better accommodation and your children will receive the finest education and healthcare. Maybe one of them will grow up to be an important officer. Not to mention the sizeable monthly salary your wife will receive. They'll never go hungry or want for anything again.'

'I trust in the good judgement and generosity of my master. They couldn't ask for a better father.'

'You can still back out…'

'I didn't know I had the choice,' said Abdel Moula in surprise.

'Such a great sacrifice can only be chosen of your own free will.'

Mourad Bey spoke with a sincerity that baffled him.

-6-

'For the family.'

So he told himself as he waited in the passage before his fight in the Colosseum. He distracted himself by trying to picture what our master looked like, to imagine what he smelled like up close, what his voice would sound like amid the roar of the baying mob, as though the image was drawn from the very depths of his desires. They had come to see Hercules slaughter his rivals; little did they know that he was to surprise them all with the day of his death.

'No. For Our Lord, rather.'

He knew now that his master's happiness was the faint thread that ran through his world, and it was stronger than any other possible motive. This love was the source of all the meanness and greatness in his heart.

He watched the piano player rehearsing with his group. In his expensive suit the pianist looked like an elegant, serious performer, but suddenly he whipped off his trousers and underwear and hunched forward to beat out the rest of the piece with his cock. It made Abdel Moula laugh a lot. He also liked the man who balanced a metal ball on the top of his foot. The top half of the ball was on fire and the man flicked it up to balance it on his head without being touched by the flames.

But best of all was the skit with the two men: one old, one young. The young man threw a bundle of ropes into the air and they turned into snakes, then the old man stepped forward and threw his stick at the snakes, and it ate them.

A delicate young man who claimed the power to bring the dead back to life: it excited Abdel Moula's sympathy. Not that he thought it was anything more than a trick, but he could appreciate any tricks the poor might play for the sake of the price of a meal.

A group of naked prisoners shuffled in, driven by the whip. From the tattoos saying *Traitor* and the yellow insignias darkening their bare skin, he could tell that they were a mix of those who had expressed doubt in the existence of the president, those who were charged with conspiracy, and those who held ideas, tendencies or habits that went against our customs and traditions as Egyptians. Abdel Moula made an obscene gesture with his middle finger and spat in their faces, full of an astonished contempt that a disease like this could still be polluting the clean air of his country.

The guards dressed their wasted bodies in fighters' loincloths, minus weapons or shields, then drove them out to the ring as a banquet for the lions. How the crowd roared to see them. He heard the words 'Our Lord' chanted over and over.

When it was time for the young man with the snakes to perform, he fixed the guards and assistants with a burning gaze and said, 'Blessed are the meek.'

Shortly afterwards, Abdel Moula heard the sound of whistles and he knew that the young man had failed to revive his snakes. Then there was fierce applause and cries, in which pain could be heard amid joy, groans amid the fervour.

The announcer's voice was stating that his fight was up next. He took a deep breath and trotted out to the ring. The crowd were whipped into a frenzy. The only name he heard was his own—'Hercules! Hercules!'—and all he could see were banners saying the same and portraits of his own face. He didn't care. All he could think about was seeing his master. And then he saw him. It was easy to spot him, and how couldn't it be? He was lit up like the sun, a king who might burn the whole world to ashes if the mood took him, without regrets, without anyone able to hold him to account.

And he was dressed as Caesar: one hand dealing punishment, the other dispensing mercy.

He saw the young resurrectionist crucified, nails through his hands and feet, a crown of thorns on his head, and blood trickling slowly down his body. He must have been ordered to perform his best tricks for the crowd after he'd failed with his snakes. The forward tilt of his bloodied head made him look like he was bowing in acknowledgement of their acclaim.

Ten powerful fighting men came into the ring, each one

armed to the teeth. The crowd wanted him to tear them to pieces with his bare hands. He picked out the strongest looking, threw him to the ground and began squeezing the man's neck between his thighs. He could have crushed the windpipe in an instant, but he was waiting for his master's signal to finish him. The mob's screams redoubled, a compelling, even seductive bond of brotherhood crying out for a decisive victory, the herd become a single body, its soul a storm, its fuel a powerful and mysterious faith. Then the signal was given and amid the crowd's fervent rejoicing, he killed the fighter.

From his cross, the resurrectionist cried, 'You are the salt of the earth, but if the salt should lose its savour then what good is it? It will be cast away and trodden underfoot.'

Now the remaining fighters surged towards him, shoulder-to-shoulder in a single formation beneath a shell of their shields, mercilessly hacking at him with their swords and hatchets. Hercules dropped. He heard the shouts of admiration change to exhortations to finish his life, to slay the champion.

'I am sending you out as a sheep among wolves, so be wise as the serpent and innocent as doves.'

Abdel Moula turned his gaze inwards. He licked his wounds and his enchanted body began to knit itself together, life rushing back into the tattered flesh until it was as though he'd never been touched. He rose like a phoenix, gave a roar, and chest bared he rushed towards them like floodwater, killing one after the other. Standing over their bundled bodies he plunged his hand into the chest of one and, giving the twist and jerk the crowd knew well, ripped out the heart. Taking a bite out of it, he then raised it aloft and waved it, not to the crowd this time, but to Our Lord, and only Our Lord.

The man on the cross cried, 'Those who take up the sword shall perish by the sword,' but this time nobody heard him.

The announcer let everybody know that the climax of his combat was yet to come:

'No matter how many Hercules has brought low, will he be able to defeat that mightiest and most unparalleled of warriors, Our Lord himself?'

Silence fell. Inside Abdel Moula, the voices of his victims began to bubble and stir and his heart quailed like a child's. This was the man he was expected to lie down for, to die for in order to take that final stride into the estate that never fell into ruins, the home that never saw hunger or want..

There was a blank disbelief in his gaze as he watched our master descend to the ring, supported by Mourad Bey. He shrugged off his robes, handed his crown to the commander, and stood there in the simple, cracked tunic of the fighter: a leather loincloth.

Abdel Moula could only wonder that this sun, which just moments before had been seated in the presidential box, should have the ruined, ugly, pitifully thin body of an old man. A nose wreathed in pimples, a face so lined it looked as though it might fall apart, and skin hanging off him like rags. A sun he could extinguish with a puff of his breath.

His faith was shaken, and it confused him. Pride and heresy filled his head like fumes risen off bad blood. How could he allow himself to be beaten by this dry twig?

'Do not test the Lord thy God.'

The crowd rose to sing the national anthem. They sung with unaccustomed enthusiasm, the words rising from the depths of hearts packed with corpses and ghosts and shadows, terror and hope. Then a great bronze gong sounded to signal that the fight had begun.

Gathering all his strength, he rushed straight for his master who, far from being flustered, stood still as a statue. But even as he reached him, Abdel Moula dropped to his knees, a servant begging forgiveness. He had made up his mind to submit. Even if he fought and killed the president, he would never escape the guard's bullets or the mob's frenzied pledge to eat the assassin alive, and his family would lose the paradise they'd been promised. A towering mountain cornered like a rat. He was hoping that by this craven submission, by placing his life in his master's hands, he might be spared.

With a gentleness that felt like a cool breeze in hell, our master stroked his head. Abdel Moula looked up and stared into the cavernous eyes, empty as dry wells, and he saw the truth.

The deal had never been that he should let his master kill him, but that he should kill his master. That through death he would loose his ageing soul from the grip of eternal life and absolute power. The man was begging him to do it. Who would truly be brave enough to kill the president with his bare hands except the true servant whose sins have been forgiven? Both men were just a pace away from paradise, from that deathless estate, and Abdel Moula alone must bear the weight of this sin with fortitude. He was facing something beyond his understanding or his capacity to explain, but the sacredness of the task had infused every atom of his being and silenced forever the incessant whine of his ghosts. He saw the shades of his victims peacefully slipping out of his soul, freeing him from years of spiritual self-loathing. Our Lord was him now, and he was Our Lord.

Like a spear, he rose up and fastened his hands round the old man's throat. He squeezed and squeezed, but as the decrepitude ran from the president's soul into his, it was as though he was the one choking. The weakness spread through his great frame, through his enchanted flesh, while the secret of his eternal life flowed into Our Lord.

Thumbs down all around the arena, and the two men broke apart like a clod of soil. But it was Our Lord who rose to his feet, a towering cliff before which the stunned crowd knelt and prayed.

The Mistake

Mohamed Kheir

Translated by Andrew Leber

HE LOOKED AROUND ANXIOUSLY to see if there were any other children in the station but found none. So he dragged Marmar behind him, trying to conceal her small body with either his own or the suitcase. She kept trying to get away from him, calling out in a high-pitched voice, which he hoped would be drowned out by the noise of the trains. Trying to evade the disdainful looks of his fellow travellers, he thought he saw a stern, middle-aged woman spit at them wordlessly, even as she turned to look away. When they finally sat down on two of the empty marble seats, he began to lecture her in a raised voice:

'Come on, my life's mistake – enough already!'

Yet these miserable attempts to feign innocence did nothing to reduce the looks of disapproval.

The justifications for having children had run out – none of them carried weight any more. Even the nurseries had closed their doors, whether due to the lack of customers or fear of public contempt. After years of general despair, a conviction had spread among society that the only resistance to the status quo was not having children, and a tacit understanding arose that considered reproduction a form of support for the political situation. Or at least approval of it.

In light of this, he began to make it clear at every opportunity that Marmar came as a mistake, whether he was chatting with acquaintances, talking to passers-by on the street or just sitting in a restaurant. But it was like screaming his innocence from the dock, repeating the same pleas all the other defendants had given, who – unfortunately for him – were all too few in number now. Sometimes, but less and less over the years, he would spot some of his counterparts pacing the streets with their heads lowered, faces fixed, as they silently pushed strollers or pulled little arms along the pavement. Though they were considered hypocrites, they obtained no official benefit from their progeny, and the official disregard for them was taken as additional evidence – handed down from on high – of their sin.

On that day, no other sinners appeared at the station. And in any case, Marmar had climbed up on his knees and started tickling his face, foiling any attempt to hide it. As the train approached, he turned to face it, but she kept trying to pull off his glasses until it had come to a halt in front of them.

They climbed into the half-full carriage. As he and Marmar took their seats, the other passengers seemed to back away, leaving them sitting as alone as they had been on the platform. From the window he could see another train going in the opposite direction, and a third passing above them. Paraphrasing Napoleon at the Pyramids, he said to himself: 'From the heights of those electric trains, a century looks down on us.' The trains formed a second sky, loaded with passengers that made up an inverted population pyramid: quiet trains overflowing with the wisdom of the elders and the concerns of the middle-aged. They were concerns he had grown used to for years until the day when Carmen shocked him with the news:

'I'm pregnant.'

THE MISTAKE

It reached him like the audio of some prehistoric television set, from a time of black-and-white and static-distorted signals. He couldn't remember ever hearing such news in his family. He grew up as the youngest of his siblings and came of age just as the wave of refusing to have children erupted, around the 80th anniversary of the January Revolution, taking root over the next two decades.

'Pregnant?!!'

She nodded.

He opened his mouth to speak and then closed it without saying anything. He turned off the phones and turned on the TV, so that ghostly images started frolicking on the wide wall of the living room. He turned up the volume, pulled Carmen close to him and spoke directly into her ear:

'How long?'

He expected that she would say a month at most, so the answer floored him:

'In the third month!'

Anger suddenly rose inside him, like a lit fuse or boiling lava, and he regretted – for a split second – that he had ever relied on her on this matter. In fact, it never occurred to him that Carmen, the leader of the childless, the enemy of children, the hater of the future, the orphan, could ever 'get involved' in a pregnancy. His cheeks reddened and he felt a little dizzy as he imagined the news spreading among his acquaintances, even as he was overcome with fear stemming from his ignorance about anything to do with children. Then he came to the subject that needed all the phones to be turned off for:

'We'll abort the baby, of course!'

He said it and fell silent. For the most part, the government did not seem to worry about combatting the wave of childlessness. It neither punished nor rewarded the childless – according to various interpretations, childlessness was fully compatible with the authorities' desire to be freed from the responsibility of providing new services. Despite that, it fought abortion by any means necessary – threatening the perpetrators – while restricting contraceptive methods. Some interpreted this as consistent with the rise of more conservative governmental tendencies which, six years before the hundredth anniversary of the revolution, had culminated in the return of the monarchy. Others cited security motives, with the government seeking to slow the rise of abject nihilism. Or perhaps they feared the imminent shift in the average age – going the way of Europeans – that threatened the labour supply for new ventures after nearly two decades of widespread childlessness.

Still, on that shocking night Carmen told him she was pregnant – a night that was now three years and ten months old – he wasn't discussing any of this, but simply trying to absorb the shock and explain the riddle: Why had Carmen got pregnant, why had she kept the pregnancy going, and why had she hidden it from him?

Her answers were unconvincing. 'I was surprised by the pregnancy and couldn't make a decision until it became too late'... 'When you're actually pregnant, as opposed to just imagining it, getting rid of it turns out to be a much harder decision'... 'I hesitated because I was afraid of what you'd say.'

None of this nonsense convinced him. He'd known her long enough to tell that the reason for her 'action' was almost certainly the convergence of stubbornness on stubbornness: stubbornness against the government, stubbornness against herself, stubbornness against him. Childlessness was no longer important, it seemed, since the government had persisted in its indifference. Actions lose their importance when practiced – or not practiced – by everyone, and so Carmen had decided to upend the lives of the two of them, soon to become three. He looked with anger – that night – at her stomach, which was not yet any bigger. He gestured with his hand – the TV turned off – gestured again – the phones turned on – and he got up and made for the bed. Even as sleep overcame him, she hadn't bothered to follow, only saying as he headed to the bedroom:

'It's a girl.'

He began to imagine – in spite of himself – a little girl wandering around the house – albeit a shadow silently crawling about, not the annoying, laughing little girl now jumping up and down in front of him as she peered through the train window. She was trying to look down at the far-off land under the criss-crossing electric train lines. He was looking at her and through the window to avoid the looks of annoyance and anger, observing her explosive vitality as he recalled the medical prognosis report at her birth: 'Potential age: 86 years.'

He knew that potential age meant 'at least' not 'maximum', and he knew that about nine decades is more than enough, especially in times of pure boredom. Still, he didn't like to think of her dying even as old as 86, twice his own age now. He imagined her living to be 100, even 200 years old. He remembers how the grey hairs had surprised him since his late twenties, and how it attracted the girls before it gave him – as he gained weight and fell into depression – years beyond his age. When he was with Marmar, he sometimes took advantage of the whiteness of his hair to evade fatherhood in the eyes of passers-by, suggesting with the heavy movements and tired eyes of a grandfather, that she was his son's fault, not his.

He would go so far as to make Marmar herself accustomed to playing with him the way cute granddaughters do, pulling on his glasses and his slight beard, asking him for sweets more than she asked him to play with her or run with her. What was his 'potential age'? He remembered the day they entered the entire country's data into a programme his friend invented – education data, the number of political parties, social diversity, class disparity – and they asked the length of time it would take before democracy or secularism were achieved. The programme spat out numbers that indicated a wait of centuries – news he rejoiced at, as it only increased his belief in childlessness. That was four years before his marriage to Carmen and nine years before she surprised him with Marmar.

Another child entered the train car! A boy, who looked about five years old – his mother wearing baggy, dark clothes – went to a far corner and sat in silence. Did the newcomers not see them? Did they see and ignore them? Was it a bigger provocation if all the children – the sins – sit in a corner together?

Could he be exaggerating? Of course not. Streets, stations and trains all looked like government offices for dealing with pensioners. Silence, Bluetooth headsets, electronic canes and prosthetic devices filled up to the horizon. He corrected himself – it all looked more like a hospital for war veterans. On the rare occasions when he saw children, it almost seemed like they were merely very short adults, the impression reinforced by the prevailing silence and stillness that their shy parents had bestowed on them.

Carmen gave birth to Marmar in the same silence, with modern tools that ensured birth was without pain and without sound as well. In the house, the infant Marmar's cries were more like screams, shattering years of silence and pounding on the eardrums of neighbours. He even installed soundproof walls for the baby's room – what used to be his office. They came and went from the building only rarely, always with apologetic body language.

It wasn't the scarcity of nurseries alone that kept them from sending Marmar to one. They loved to sit with her, and Carmen's maternity leave and his remote work as a translator allowed them to. It also kept them from admitting that they had now been expelled from their social circles, tarred as liars, pretenders, and hypocrites who promoted ideas they didn't adhere to. It also kept him from admitting that – in various

THE MISTAKE

indirect ways – he blamed Carmen for the situation. It would be fair to say that they increasingly stayed in the house, not just out of love for Marmar, but also because there was no longer a difference between passers-by who were disgusted by their child, and former friends of their nihilistic struggle. Indeed, these comrades were even harder on them. Was it that blame, and his gradual abandonment of Carmen, that drove her to do what she did?

It felt a little funny to use the phrase 'do what she did', because he didn't really know anything about 'what she did'. He might even say he didn't have a clue about anything his wife did any more. He saw her fall silent, become lost in thought, go off by herself, but presumed it was because she blamed herself and that she deserved it. Then one day she went out alone and did not return. Her phone did not answer. The night crept in quickly between the trains criss-crossing in the sky, and before he went out to search for her, they had arrived.

They searched the house with optical and sonar scanning devices, all kinds of electronic devices. They did it all in silence after they made him and Marmar sit below the wall where the television's ghosts played. They did not ask him any questions and they did not answer any of his. He knew that they wouldn't. They left with the same calm they arrived with and never returned. Neither did Carmen, not for the last eighteen months. Since that night, he had been under surveillance, too – additional surveillance. Now he had to pay attention to his behaviour on the internet, as they monitored him with algorithms that could piece together the motives that led to any accumulation of web searches. He had to keep his calm for the sake of Marmar, since it wasn't her fault. Now, like all the mistakes of his life, he had to learn to love her as much as he could.

The electric train came to a halt at the final station. 'Come on, Marmar,' he called to her, and she jumped down from the seat next to the window. He pulled the wheeled suitcase and held the little girl's hand. They exited the train and began descending the endless escalators, taking a few long minutes to reach ground level. They exited the station to the square, which was wide, cool, and bright. The breeze stirred the flags scattered around the pavements and shop entrances – flags emblazoned with the three famous colours, now with the royal crown returned to replace the golden eagle. He remembered that this was once a royal square, and now had returned to another royal in another time just a few years before the anniversary of the revolution that took place right here. Why did the new king want to tie himself to the revolution? Neither he nor his father nor probably even his grandfather had been alive to see it, the last one before the 'End of the Era of Revolutions.'

The term sounded similar to the phrase 'End of the Dynastic Era' that he learned while studying the pharaohs in school. The pharaohs' dynasties never returned, nor did the revolutions, but could other, non-pharaonic families return? Perhaps other revolutions too, just not the kind that took place in public squares? He realised he had reached the point where his analysis of the world was based on chance connections between words and phrases, and that it was complete madness. He noticed Marmar pointing to an ice cream shop that must be more than 200 years old, a century older than the pain that befell the square. They ate ice cream on their way to Nana's house.

His mother welcomed them, holding a pair of antique knitting needles in her hands – the family's heirloom. She was making summer sweaters for him and the little girl, as if she were greeting them straight out of the past. She looked with amazement and cautious enthusiasm at the suitcase, and asked:

'Are you finally coming to stay with me?'

He made sure that the little girl was preoccupied with the antique, flat TV, and answered:

THE MISTAKE

'Marmar will stay with you.'

'And you? Where are you going?'

He paused for a moment and adjusted his words:

'I mean, she will stay with you. I may come back tonight or tomorrow.'

She knew he wouldn't say anything more – stubborn like his father and like his poor, vanished wife. She set out the lunch, not forgetting the fried potatoes for the little one. He only ate some rice, as his stomach had been hurting since he'd first arrived. He got up, kissed his mother, looked at Marmar while trying hard not to well up, then left the house. The winter sun was somehow bright and subdued at the same time. The old streets, once decorated with trees in the autumn, now dazzled metallically with signs, barriers, and the electric train lines suspended in the sky. He was amazed that any of the sun's rays managed to reach them at all through such crowded skies. At night, the spaces between the elevated trains would pulse with the lights of laser-drawn advertisements...

First, he crossed the square in the direction of the Nile, standing on the Corniche and looking at the waves of grey water ready to welcome winter. The river seemed more powerful than the pedestrians on its banks. He walked south towards old Garden City, crossing the road again and heading into the quiet alleys among the ancient palaces, stirring up vivid memories of those first days with Carmen. He remembered picnics and fleeting kisses. He thought about how everything was afflicted by modernisation except love – love remained the same.

Garden City grew quieter and quieter as he walked in the almost-deserted, wintery street, crossing Qasr Al-Aini Street towards Al-Muneera. He passed through a crowd for a short while until he reached the fruit market, stopping on the corner of Mansour Street to contemplate the dim yellow light of the lampposts. The government employees had all left their offices for the day, leaving the windows open for the air to stir the papers they left behind. A strange feeling came over him for a moment, as though he were going back in time. He thought that time itself might slow wherever there were employees or government agencies. Still, he continued on to Al-Muneera, looking at the old building with its huge dark gates. He approached quietly, catching a glimpse of the guard towers but not who was inside them, while a soldier looked at him indifferently. The gate drew near, and a man in civilian clothes with an automatic weapon stopped him and asked in a quiet, strict voice:

'Where are you headed?'

'I want my wife.'

The Sky Room

Azza Sultan

Translated by Elisabeth Jaquette

THE SKY HADN'T ALWAYS been so grey, or maybe it had been, and I'd just never noticed. The memories I hold on to suggest the sky did once have a colour: a constant blue, with clouds shaped by our imaginations – this one looked like an elephant, that one looked like my father's profile, and another like a rabbit on the verge of running.

We would sit in a room on the seventieth floor designated for touching the sky, and that's what we called it: the Sky Room. The room was made entirely of glass, down to the walls and ceiling, a thrilling adventure for whoever managed to go up there. My teacher used to say that going to the room gave us a new kind of confidence, but accidents did happen, regularly, to children who wanted to fly, and safety measures weren't as strict as we first thought. Seil, the girl who used to play word games with me every week, fell from up there, and Ghafir took flight when he tried to grab hold of a cloud that looked like a bicycle he'd seen in an old movie, wishing he could have one like it.

Eventually, we were forbidden from going up to the Sky Room unless we were with our families. My father, however, always preferred the earth. He eagerly anticipated the time each week when we were allowed to walk through the streets, and when it arrived, he would go outside, take off his shoes, and let his feet touch the pavement. I would laugh and copy him, saying, 'Father, I want to hold a cloud,' and he would tell me that clouds emanate from the earth, that they are secret messages from the earth to the sky.

My father used old-fashioned phrases like the ones in his books, old-fashioned like the objects he held onto until the building management forbade him from using them.

The sky is dark now, devoid of clouds, and the earth is littered with the rubble of high-rise buildings. My little girl knows nothing of what came before. She cries all the time that she wants food, so I use a little flour to make bread, and hope it lasts until the plane arrives with provisions for the week.

They made the floor of the room look like the sky, while the walls and ceiling were made of glass. If we won the weekly competitions, artificial intelligence gave us virtual clouds to hug and take pictures with.

Going up there with my family became as much a fixture as one of the room's walls and had its downsides. My mother would reminisce about going out with her friends, and the places that once existed but were removed for the New Republic's sake. My mother never tired of these stories, and some of the women who were there to keep us from touching the sky would join in; they always chatted while we kept quiet and daydreamed.

One day, Mrs. Mais told us that her grandmother had once taken part in one of the revolutions, and my mother added that her grandmother had too. I'd been having no luck touching the clouds, so I eavesdropped on their conversation instead. My mother inherited many stories from my grandmother, but she never told us any where she was the hero, except for the one where she married my father. Now she was recounting a protest once held when the pyramids were to be removed; my mother was a teenager at the time and she went with my grandmother. Her eyes filled with tears at this story. Mrs. Mais fell silent and then they changed the subject. I'd never seen these pyramids; they must have been removed in the end. It wasn't until I was older that I understood why my mother was sad, why her eyes filled with tears: their protest had failed.

My mother and Mrs. Mais returned to their grandmothers' stories, and my mother laughed and said how much she missed a dish she called mahshi. She didn't know why she couldn't seem to make it any more; the vegetables she needed were available, more or less, but somehow it wasn't the same. Their conversations often began with laughter but quickly turned to sadness, sometimes even to tears scarcely visible in my mother's eyes. Is this what nostalgia does to us?

It sparks, and our souls brew a storm of tears that stream from our eyes and extinguish the fires kindled by loss? How cruel nostalgia can be!

My daughter is crying. She must be hungry, and time passes slowly. My husband didn't bring back much firewood, barely enough for three or four loaves of bread. We just need one loaf now, to fill the maw of the hunger monster that's been unleashed and pursues me.

I consider baking bread over the fire. How can we make bread without yeast? They forgot to put yeast in the supply bags. I should tell the official next week, but his plane can't touch down, the ground isn't suitable, it barely comes close enough to drop containers near our tents. The relief committees are trying to save as many of us as they can.

I hug my daughter, hoping she'll quiet down.

My father would walk barefoot and say he's lucky, holding my hand and telling me, 'We were a country of civilisation.'

'Father, we *are* a country of civilisation,' I would reply, and he would laugh and say civilisation is more than bridges and tall buildings. My father told me about an old building called the

Tower; once he went to the top floor with his father and gazed across the city with a telescope. I asked him whether the Tower was as tall as our building, and he said our building is taller but we can't see anything from the top – all the other buildings have glass facades, and in a mirror you see nothing but yourself.

I never understood my father when he spoke about mirrors. He said they're deceptive, that they don't show the truth, only what we want to see, so we don't recognise our flaws and never try to change them. We grow accustomed to our faults, and each one of us loves who we see in the mirror. 'We've become *selfish*,' he added, saying the word in English. 'You mean self-centred?' I asked, repeating in Arabic. My father laughed and said, 'Yes, someone who is selfish loves himself, and wants everything for himself.' I told my father he wasn't selfish, he loved me and my mother. He picked me up and hugged me tightly, then lifted me as high as his arms could reach and placed me back on the ground. With a smile, he said, 'Of course I love you and your mother, but mirrors ruin us.'

'Father, I don't understand,' I told him. He fell silent and quickened his pace. He told me of a temple where the ceiling encompassed the heavens, and I asked him, 'Like the Sky Room?'

'No, that's just the sky,' my father said.

'Father, what's a temple?' He talked and talked, and when I grew tired of repeating, 'Father, I don't understand,' again and again, I let him continue talking and retreated to my dreams. *Who was in the Sky Room now*, I wondered?

My father wished we were permitted to walk through the streets more than one day a week, but in our city it was just one. Once, he travelled to another city with three friends to join their day for walking, but when he returned, he was forbidden from walking in our city for three weeks. At the time my father said he was being framed, what reason did he have to travel to another city? Networks broadcast my father's actions and punishment, and he was famous for the next six hours. Several channels offered him large sums of money to

THE SKY ROOM

appear and talk about what he did, but he wasn't permitted to discuss it. My father turned down a large fortune.

Before the decree that our families had to accompany us to the Sky Room, I used to go up there with my friend Tina, and we would give the clouds names. We had a way of making the sky change colours; once I turned it green and made the clouds orange, so when it rained it would look like orange juice, which I loved so much. Or maybe carrot juice, since carrots are orange too? Tina ignored me and turned the clouds purple, like bruises, and when this made me angry, she changed the sky black and laughed. The room was filled with other boys and girls, and every minute the sky flashed different shades, each one of us making it our favourite colour.

We would keep turning the sky different colours until we forgot what colour it was supposed to be. Then Farid would restart it and the sky would go back to its original shade, the blue I now love. At that age I didn't like blue; when the colours fluctuated, they were reflected across all the mirrors, but when the sky was blue, so was everything else, and it looked so boring. My mother told me the sea was blue too, but I'd never seen the sea, it was far away and the only way we could visit was by submitting an application and being put on the visitor list.

One day, our turn came, and we took a trip to the coast. We were allowed six square metres in which to swim, but they said there were wild sea creatures out there. I didn't know why my father was so enchanted with the sea, our building's swimming pools and exercise areas were all larger than those six square metres they permitted us. I wasn't a confident swimmer, I felt nervous and scared, and after two attempts I got out of the water, changed my clothes, and contented myself with watching.

My father didn't even enter the water, let alone swim. Instead he reached down, took a handful of water, and swallowed it. My mother laughed at this, but my father looked at her and said, 'This is all that's left of my parents.'

In the five days we spent by the sea, my father kept drinking seawater and using it to bathe, but he never swam in it. He would put on his swimsuit, walk along the beach, bury his toes in the sand, take a deep breath, and close his eyes. My father loved monotony and repetition. I didn't enjoy our trip at all; the sky felt far away, as did the clouds, and the sea wasn't the friend my father had told me about. I tried to copy my father and drink seawater, but it was too salty and I couldn't make myself swallow it, no matter how determined I was. My father must have been very determined, enough to do it five times.

My daughter's crying fades, and I look at her and realise she's fallen asleep. The bread is finally done, and I don't know whether to wake her for food or let her keep sleeping while I finish the other loaves. My indecision gives way to my impulse to wake her; bread tastes much better fresh, good enough to be eaten by itself, and the relief committee only gave us one container of cheese, not enough for the three of us. They say there are lots of survivors, but in my area there can't be more than a hundred families, and a few girls and boys without parents.

My daughter begins to eat and I'm struck by memories from the night of the collapse. The buildings looked like playing cards; when you nudge one, the rest fall down, one after the other. Hundreds of suspension bridges and thousands of tall buildings collapsed so easily. How had we survived?

Father saved us... Father. All that's left of him are his stories, memories we had of us together, and the habit he passed down to me of walking barefoot. We were lucky; eventually we were permitted to walk outside every day. Studies revealed that staying inside all day – living and working always indoors – drove many people to suicide, so the government amended its regulations to allow people to walk every day. It even created open areas dedicated exclusively for walking. Regulations still prohibited more than three people from walking together, and this my father adhered to closely. His love for consistency surpassed everything else. My mother didn't accompany us every time, she often went with a friend to do the shopping, and I only walked with my father four days a week because sometimes he wanted to walk with his two friends. Regulations also forbade anyone from having more than two friends, and I liked knowing lots of people, so from time to time I would pick new friends. My father laughed at me, and said, 'You don't know what friendship means.' He told me that if I found someone who loved and accepted me the way I was, I shouldn't abandon them.

'Father, I don't understand,' I said.

He smiled and said, 'You'll grow up, you'll understand.'

I was walking with my husband and daughter when we saw the bridges collapse, then the buildings; it felt like a dream. We didn't know what was happening, we didn't understand. Maybe it was a trick, or a new experiment they were doing. We stood there, watching it all without speaking. I don't know what happened to us. Now we're somewhere far away, maybe in the outlying deserts.

You saved us, Father, just as you always did. I wish I'd understood what you were saying at the time; comprehension came much later for me, too late to reach you or show you I understand. I have nothing left of you. When you died, we had to surrender your body to the public hospital, and they took your organs to give to those in need. Father, they say that our country is the largest exporter of organs in the world. Medical tourism has become very popular, and certain organs must be transplanted quickly, so patients come here and wait for a suitable person to die. Maybe your eyes are providing sight for two people I'll never meet. Maybe your heart is beating in someone else's body. Can you imagine, Father, if this law had been in effect during the revolution that Grandfather participated in, how many young people who lost an eye in the clashes would have regained their ability to see?

The problem is that solutions always come too late. Before the collapse, I visited the National Archives often to look at photographs of you and us, and videos we took together. You know, Father, that we were only permitted to keep one photograph each year. I wasted so many opportunities, enthralled with the pictures in the Sky Room.

It was there that I learned what it felt like to touch a cloud. I actually touched one, Father, it wasn't an artificial intelligence trick. I reached into a mass of cold water droplets, the vapour was very dense. I didn't actually grab the cloud – how could someone grab vapour, even if it seems solid in front of us? – but I touched it. My mother managed to strike a deal with the official on duty that day, she gave him one of her 'treasures', as Grandmother used to call them, the old flag. Grandmother had made it and given it to mother as a good luck charm before she passed away, telling her not to waste it. My mother made sure to keep it hidden, so it wouldn't be taken from her and placed in the National Archives, she told me. The official's eyes widened when my mother spoke to him, and he immediately agreed. It wasn't until many years later that my mother told me what she'd done. At the time, I didn't think much of it, I just hugged her for a long time.

Tina responded in kind, Father. She exchanged me for other friends. I had begun to follow your advice, feeling she could be a lifelong friend, when she sent me an email informing me that the place she had occupied was now vacant. She'd met someone new, who she could imagine being friends with for a long time.

I started going to the Sky Room alone, content to spend the full moon days chatting with it and telling it stories about you, my mother, and my grandparents. Did my grandmother and grandfather first meet in the Square, I wonder? Or had they been friends before? You forgot to tell me, Father, and aside from a few lines, I can't find anything about that revolution or the ones before it. I keep reciting your stories, afraid of forgetting, afraid of losing them before I can pass them on to my daughter.

They say, Father, that we accomplished what generations

for thousands of years before us had not. Buildings reached into the sky, and new developments were everywhere. It's true, of course, that the river dried up, but the administration was sensible and able to deal with it. Now the river ends in a lake in the south of the country; we can see the area on virtual trips, but it's filled with crocodiles and all sorts of other reptiles, so visiting in person is prohibited.

The older I got, the less often I went to the Sky Room, even though our families were no longer required to accompany us once we turned thirteen. I missed Tina a lot and didn't find it easy to make new friends. I'm not sure whether it really was hard, or whether I simply lost the desire to seek them out. I passed time gazing at my reflection in the mirror. As a teenager, even going for walks no longer appealed to me.

Tina's place remained vacant for years, until one day she sent me an email asking if I had an opening for a friend. No one had taken her place, Father, but I sent her my regrets. I don't know why. I feared my inherited attachment to the sea and earth, I saw myself longing to go walking as if it were a rendezvous with a lover.

I didn't make another close friend like Tina until I met the man who would be my daughter's father.

When my mother became ill, there were no dead whose organs she could be offered, but when she died we still sent her body to the public hospital so that it migth help others. You refused to remarry, Father, despite all the emails you received from the city government about suitable women your age.

The sound of fire blends with the smell and travels up my nostrils until I cry. A loaf burned and I didn't notice. Our chances of having anything to eat are growing slimmer, and my husband hasn't come home yet. I go look through the relief bag, and at the bottom I'm surprised to see not a container of powdered milk or packets of yeast, but a jar of fruit preserves. I shout for joy, so loud I nearly wake my daughter.

I step outside the tent and leap into the air, barely containing my glee. I feel like I can actually touch the air, and I leap up again and again until my foot lands on a small rock. The pain rivals my joy so I go back inside, and decide to bake a cake. We have a few clay baking dishes – my husband and the other men made them and distributed them equally among us, though if any family needs a bigger one or an additional one for some reason, we all help them out. I've gotten to know many women here, since there are no rules about the number of friends a person can have. My husband goes with at least five other men to explore the area around us, and when they get tired, they return, collecting firewood on their way; I always need wood for the fire.

Yeast makes a difference with dough. I inhale the scent and see my father.

My parents were eager to recount all the tales they'd heard from their parents. When I was young, I complained; I didn't like their stories and just wanted to go to the Sky Room. When my father accompanied me, he never stopped talking, he said that telling stories is how we preserve history. 'Father, why do we need history,' I had asked, and he said that everything has a history, even clouds were ancient from a certain perspective.

'Father, I don't understand.'

My father had hugged me and asked which cloud looked like him; I picked one and said, 'That cloud looks like your profile, Father.' He laughed and kept talking as I gazed up at the sky, not understanding.

I finish the batter and wait for my husband to come home with the wood so we can bake the cake. I lie on my back and observe the sky, a sky devoid of clouds. The smell of the batter fills my nose, and the sound of my father telling stories hangs in my ears, the way he would laugh when I said 'Father, I don't understand.' I reach out my hand to sketch my father in the sky, and an image of him as a young man appears, before changing into the way he looked before he died. I smile, and tell him,

'Father, I understand now.'

Encounter with the White Rabbit

Michel Hanna

Translated by Mohammed Ghalayini

IT HAD BEEN TEN long years since he last visited Cairo. Ever since the flood, the situation there had been getting more and more dangerous. But today he had no choice. It was a matter of life or death: the journey might well be his last hope.

The monorail had stopped going into Cairo quite a while ago. The last stop now was at the gates of the Capital. He got off and went down the stairs with the others, then headed towards the city gate. He was the only one heading that way, being the only one crazy enough to risk going out there. At the gate, he was questioned by guards who then made a copy of his ID card and Capital residency permit before letting him on his way. It was a routine procedure as there were no restrictions on leaving. Coming into the Capital, on the other hand, required special permission. He went through the first gate, then a second, then a third. A gate in each of the three walls surrounding the Capital, each of different height and separated by its own buffer zone. At each stage he was subjected to the same procedures until, finally, he was out.

His whole body was trembling with anticipation. After all the horrifying stories he'd heard about life outside the Capital, he was expecting to be jumped on and murdered the moment he set foot outside. But it wasn't so. He certainly hadn't expected all the hustle and bustle beyond the walls, or to be greeted by a vast expanse of sand teeming with people. There were tea stalls and tents, vehicle repair workshops, hawkers peddling their wares, and hundreds of flying tuktuks ready to transport anyone anywhere. These small vehicles hovered a metre above the ground and had enough room onboard for two passengers and the driver. They were so called after the three-wheeled Indian tuktuks that were common in Egypt in the 21st century. He remembered there were workers coming in and out of the Capital every day because they weren't allowed to spend the night there, so of course there would be a community outside the gates to serve these workers and transport them.

'The airport?' asked the young, dark-skinned man – a driver looking for a customer. He froze for a moment, then collected himself and told the driver he wanted to go to Heliopolis. The man explained he needed to go to the airport first, and from there he could catch another tuktuk wherever he wanted. He hesitated for a moment then agreed and followed the young man for a short distance across the sandy terrain to an area with a large number of tuktuks. The sun was scorching and the air was humid; the faintest movement would stir clouds of dust that clogged his nose. The young man boarded one of the tuktuks and he climbed in behind him. The vehicle rose and set off immediately, leaving a dust storm in its wake.

The rush of air cooled him a little and dried his sweat. They flew over the sand, taking no particular route, surrounded by tens of similar vehicles going in all directions across the desert. He was amazed at how the driver knew where to go. To think that in the previous century, the government spent billions paving thousands of kilometres of roads, only for these hovercrafts to come along, gliding on a cushion of compressed air, and negating the need for roads. Or any of that asphalt they laid. All that money gone to waste!

In the distance, the sun reflected off an eyesore of corrugated-tin huts. Row upon row, seemingly with no end. The vehicle closed in fast and skirted the edges of this settlement, finally coming to rest in a vast lot filled with thousands of tuktuks and tens of thousands of people randomly coming and going while drivers called out their destinations through deafening loudhailers. The driver looked round, waiting for his passenger to get out.

'Is this the airport?' he asked.

The driver raised an eyebrow, mockingly: 'Is his highness a tourist here?'

He was expecting to see airplanes and terminal buildings, or anything indicating the existence of an airport. But Cairo International Airport had stopped operating decades ago and the whole area was now a refuge for transients and a place for tuktuks to gather.

A sense of danger came upon him. He felt exposed by his accent, exposed by his mannerisms, exposed by his ignorance. He didn't belong here; he belonged in the cloistered Capital. If anyone figured this out, his life would be at risk. Anything could happen.

Rather than betray even more of his ignorance by asking what the fare was, he simply handed the driver a 5000 EGP note, and waited for the change, expecting the ride to cost much less. But the driver pocketed the note, didn't look back, and said, 'Out you get'.

The craft was still about a metre above the ground. Shouldn't the driver lower it a little first? he wondered. He hesitated and thought to ask him how he should get down, then decided against it and just jumped off, at which the driver took off immediately, leaving him to be engulfed in a cloud of dust that filled his eyes and nose. He coughed and sputtered and rubbed his eyes. He spent close to five minutes shaking the dust out of his hair and clothes. Did the driver do this on purpose? It might be prudent to talk as little as possible from now on, he thought.

He looked around. The sun blazed oppressively overhead and the air was thick with the stench of sweat, rot, dirt and vehicle grease. The din of the crowd and the loudspeakers was deafening. He couldn't make out a word of what was being said. It was as if space itself was screaming incessantly. He felt light-headed, as if he were about to faint.

Sitting down, he covered his ears and took a deep breath of dusty air which in turn caused him to start coughing. Feeling close to suffocation, he stood up again and noticed a bustle of people around what seemed like a fight. Curiosity getting the better of him, he went over to get a closer look. Two drivers were arguing and shouting insults at each other. One of them pulled out what looked like a knife while the other pulled out what appeared to be a firearm; it was hard to tell from where he stood. He began to panic; it seemed like someone would be butchered to death in an instant. There was no sign of any police, indeed there was no government. The central government had abandoned these areas many years ago and stopped offering any services whatsoever. These days, government services were the preserve of the Capital and ten other walled cities. Outside of them, it was up to you to take care of yourself. At that moment, he saw a hulk of a man burst through the crowd, shouting and frothing, and the two drivers stopped their fight immediately. He remembered reading about how the futuwwa system of the early twentieth century was making a comeback; people needed some way to keep order. It's not like anyone consciously decided to put these ad hoc systems of justice into place. These structures just appear spontaneously wherever there is a need, just like they developed in human societies hundreds of years ago.

He let the enforcement run its course and decided to make a move. He didn't have time for this. He looked at the chaotic scenes surrounding him and struggled to understand how people found their way around this place and how they knew what to ride to get to where they wanted to go. Maybe he needed to ask someone.

Cautiously, he asked a passing pedestrian who told him he needed to find a tuktuk with a yellow sticker on it. Approaching one such vehicle, he carefully asked about his destination and its cost. He got in, and the tuktuk rose and set off.

His contact had sent him coordinates for their meeting point on his mobile. There is no cellular network coverage outside the city walls: why would there be? The internet could always be accessed through satellites, which was how people outside the walls communicated. Fortunately, these satellites were all under foreign ownership. The only problem – apart from the high cost – was that there was no way to pay the subscription fee to these companies electronically out here. Instead, some people with foreign credit cards use them to make payments for others and charge a fee equivalent to the cost of an entire subscription. This is how things go; if you want it you have to pay.

The agreed meeting place was by the Basilica of the Holy Virgin in Heliopolis, one of very few buildings to have survived from the old times. At some point, the Government decided to protect heritage sites with reinforced glass to prevent anyone from getting in. By contrast, most of buildings of its age had been demolished over the years. He'd seen pictures of old buildings on the internet, but now only a fraction of what had been there a few generations ago remained.

The tuktuk weaved its way between residential towers that looked like ruins, and ruins that looked like residential towers. Millions of people were crammed into these spaces. There seemed to be no room for any more; a real hell. People had been moving south ever since the Delta started sinking into the Mediterranean. It started with seawater flooding into Damietta, Edku, Port Said and Rashid. Then little by little it crept further inland. In the space of five years, the water was half a metre above the ground and the four cities were almost empty; their populations having migrated southward, with most people headed to Cairo, just as many buildings there were starting to crumble and collapse. Another five years passed and the water rushed in even faster till it reached Damanhour, Kafr El-Shaikh and Mansoura, and then on to El-Mahalla and Tanta. Problems also arose in Alexandria, which had initially withstood the flood because the authorities had protected its shoreline with great blocks of concrete and wave breaks. The mass migration accelerated, causing total chaos in Cairo. Displaced people put up tents wherever there was an inch of space: on the roads, on pavements, under bridges. When the overcrowding escalated, people forced their way into empty apartments and took over buildings that were still under construction, but even this was not enough. There were thousands of families living on the streets in their cars. Squabbles, fights and violent incidents broke out daily. There were thousands of murders and hundreds of thousands of robberies. Then came the great famine. After Egypt's 'food basket', the Delta's agricultural land, fell under water, and crops and livestock were greatly affected. What followed were scenes that could have been described by Maqrizi[1] in his history books; repeated, almost word for word. Indeed people started to refer to events as 'the new Mustansirian hardship'.

The government completely lost control of the situation. Dead bodies were everywhere; cities reeked with the stench of rotting flesh, sweat and death. People started targeting the police and government buildings to express their rage at how the authorities' chronic failures. This was how government services began to recede. This was still nothing compared to the real chaos that came with the 2101 earthquake. Its epicentre was off the coast of Alexandria and it brought about a tsunami that broke the sea walls and swept away what was left of Alexandria. The water continued its march inland till it reached Al Khankah, Miyyet Nimma and Imbabah. Greater Cairo was now on the shores of the Mediterranean. That year, the same plight befell the cities by the Red Sea. This time it wasn't long before Suez, Ain Sokhna, Hurghada, El Qoseir, Marsa Alam and the rest of the southern coastal towns and cities started to sink. The only things standing in its way were the Red Sea Mountains.

Millions died that year, either from the tsunami or the chaos from the mass displacement and the search for land fit for life.

The tuktuk driver snapped him out of his trance when he brought the vehicle down and asked him to get off. He looked around him and couldn't see any of the landmarks of Heliopolis that he knew from old photos. Concrete lumps teetered skywards, and the streets were filled with tents and tin shacks.

'Where's the Basilica?' he asked.

The driver waved his hand in some vague direction, 'You've got to walk from here,' he said. 'There's no road.' He got down and started walking in that direction. He was still not used to the putrid smell and was breathing with difficulty as he passed amongst the tents, trying his best not to bump into anyone or make eye contact. He walked for a long time and became unsure if he was even going in the right direction. Then, suddenly, at a distance like a bashful dwarf amongst the skyscrapers, it appeared. The reinforced glass was gone, although the metal pillars to which the glass was fixed were still there. The hordes had broken through the glass a while ago and used the building for shelter, although nobody back in the Capital knew of this.

He went as close to the building as the throng allowed. Now, he had to find the White Rabbit. This was the alias of the person who, he had been told, could supply him with Gigadol.

His wife was dying. She had Stage Three cancer and was close to death. Gigadol was the only effective treatment for cancer, but it was scarce at the best of times and hadn't been available for years. The world had been plunged into chaos since the ice caps melted and tsunamis had ravaged different coasts. Supplies of this miracle cure had run out, even for the residents of the Capital. All his life savings were only enough to buy two ampoules, but two ampoules were all he needed. And the White Rabbit, he had been told, was the man who could supply it.

At the bottom of Alexandria's sunken harbour there lies an old ship on the seabed containing a shipment of Gigadol in the hold. Hundreds upon hundreds of precious, healing ampoules. Only the White Rabbit knows the exact spot where the ship lies and he has been able to dive down and retrieve its treasure. Even though the ampoules are now over ten years old they are still effective. They may have lost ten percent of their efficacy but this will not make a big difference. Sealed inside its glass containers, the medicine lies safe, from all the surrounding seawater. Or so he has been told.

It all sounds convincingly reasonable but it is still hard to imagine what someone with all these skills might look like. The White Rabbit could be one person or a gang of many. Yes, it must be the name of a gang, he thought.

He drew closer to one of the buildings and leaned against a wall. It was as if he was afraid that someone would snatch his phone if he took it out of his pocket. He carefully took his phone out and sent a message via the satellite internet to the agreed number. The message would allow the White Rabbit to pinpoint his location. The next few minutes dragged like an eternity. Was he near or would he be coming from far away? Would he even come at all?

Fifteen minutes or so later he saw a tall man wearing sunglasses and a dark cap approaching him. The man got his phone out, looked at the screen then looked at him. He put his phone back in his pocket and ordered, 'Follow me.'

He then turned away and walked briskly. They could not do the exchange on the street. It had to be a safer place, as I later learned. The man had a wide stride and walked fast so it was exhausting to keep up with him. He had to rush after him, worried he might lose him. The man walked without stopping for close to half an hour, and then dipped into a tight passage between two buildings. There, in an open courtyard, he took the cover off a modern hovercraft.

'Get in,' the White Rabbit ordered.

This was the first time he had seen a hovercraft like this. It was the type that could fly around eight metres off the ground and rise above the bustle where the tuktuks flew. Imports of this type are not allowed and their use is prohibited, even for the residents of the Capital, for security reasons, even though they are very common in other countries. Out here though, where there is no law, anyone can get whatever they want as long as they can pay the price. A cost that surpasses the actual price many times over, of course.

He got onto the hovercraft with the White Rabbit. It rose gently upwards till they were out of the building's courtyard and they set off.

The hovercraft flew on a cushion of air that was bigger and more pressurised than that of any tuktuk, so it caused turbulence and disturbance to any craft that crossed underneath it. Simply passing over a vehicle caused it to have an accident. The White Rabbit caused so many accidents on their flight and he didn't even care to look.

He looked around him, contemplating. There were no clear landmarks that he recognised; only crowds and towering, sun-bleached buildings as far as the eye could see. Finally a familiar structure, the 6th of October Bridge, a flyover that cuts all the way across Cairo. He'd seen it on his last visit to Cairo a decade before. Most of the bridge sections had collapsed and all that remained were the pillars of concrete. As they approached the swamps of downtown Cairo, the weather became less dry and the heat more bearable. The craft hovered above the watery stretches between ruins, leaving a misty cloud. One building that wasn't in ruins but rather well preserved caught his eye. He got his phone out and turned the camera towards the building to bring up its details:

> DAVIES BRYAN BUILDING
> Constructed: 1910
> Designer: Robert Williams

He noticed another building that was still standing amongst the ruins but he couldn't make out its details.

Downtown Cairo and its historic neighbourhoods were the first to succumb to ruin, though this had nothing to do with climate change or sea levels. The cause, in this case, was groundwater which had made the area uninhabitable over 40 years ago. At first, water started seeping into basements then rose year on year till the ground floors were uninhabitable. This was the reason for the intense overcrowding in areas like Heliopolis and Nasr City, Mokattam Mountain and the neighbourhoods of New Cairo City in the east and the Pyramids Plateau in the west. There was just so little dry land left.

The craft continued hovering over the patchwork of water and ruins for some time. He spotted some small boats passing down erstwhile streets; it looked like there was a small community living on the water in downtown Cairo. Finally, the craft approached the remains of a massive, partially collapsed, but still inhabitable, building. It suddenly dawned on him: this was the Mogamma of Tahrir Square! Just to be sure, he got his phone out and checked with the camera. It really was the Mogamma! This meant the huge space of open water in front of it was once Tahrir Square. Exactly a century ago, right here, hundreds of thousands of people gathered, shaking the sky and the buildings with their angry voices. The sky was still there but the buildings were now just watery ruins. The question was: what happened to all that rage.

In one of the corners of the Mogamma, somewhere around the third floor, there was a huge opening, wide enough for the craft to land in, and so they did. It took a while for his eyes to adjust to the difference in light levels between here and the outside. The door opened, the White Rabbit got out and he followed.

The floor where they had landed looked like it had been converted into a warehouse. Row upon row of shelves were fixed to the walls with assorted contents. There were also boxes all over the floor. The White Rabbit stopped by one of the shelves and turned away. Was this just a secret warehouse or did he live here too?

Curiously he approached one of the boxes to take a look.

'Don't touch anything!' the White Rabbit ordered.

'What is this place? Is it safe?'

'Don't worry, the building is stable.'

'Why have we stopped here? Aren't we going to Alexandria?'

'Why would we go to Alexandria?'

'Aren't we going to dive to the ship for the Gigadol ampoules?'

The White Rabbit couldn't contain his laughter, which reverberated around the place like the ringing of bells.

'We retrieved the ampoules a long time ago. Do you seriously think I'm going to dive for them every time someone needs one or two ampoules?'

The White Rabbit reached for a peculiar device that looked like an old electronic payment terminal, but much thicker. It had a long antenna suggesting it could communicate with satellites.

'You have to transfer the money now.'

With a few taps and swipes on the device, all his life savings would be transferred to the White Rabbit's account –

presumably a foreign account as electronic transactions weren't allowed outside the walled cities where the government still rules.

'Won't you show me the medicine first?'

The White Rabbit took two ampoules out of his pocket and offered them for inspection. It all felt too easy. He took the ampoules and got his phone and directed the camera towards them. The details came up on the screen:

> GIGADOL
> Active ingredient: Vendoclavicin, 12.5mg/ml
> Spectroscopic analysis: NO MATCH

Is the medicine counterfeited? Is it a scam? Could the phone have identified the medicine simply from the text on the sticker, but then realised the colour of the liquid does not match what is known for Gigadol?

'This isn't Gigadol!'

The White Rabbit responded sarcastically, 'What is it then?'

'I don't know, but my phone says it isn't Gigadol.'

'The phone is wrong.'

'The phone is never wrong; it ran a spectroscopic analysis of the fluid and it doesn't match.'

'It's normal for the colour to change. This ampoule is more than ten years old. It's expired. Of course it will deviate a little from the standard.'

The White Rabbit sounds convincing, but how can he be sure? He can't give him all his money for goods that are suspect. What if he loses everything and the medicine turns out to be fake? What then? What hope would be left for him and his wife?

He felt his head spin and his heart rate rise. He ran the analysis again:

> Spectroscopic analysis: NO MATCH

No, he couldn't risk it. He needed to look elsewhere. Surely the White Rabbit wasn't the only one who can secure rare and banned substances.

He handed the ampoules back over to the White Rabbit. 'I don't want it,' he said.

'As you wish.'

The White Rabbit took the ampoules and presented the payment device again.

'You now have to pay half the amount we agreed upon.'

'Why? I haven't taken anything from you!'

'To cover the cost of the trip, the security issues, the fuel cost, my time, and the exposure to risk. None of it's free, you know.'

'But…' His voice trailed off.

The White Rabbit's face was serious, he wasn't joking.

'It's too much!'

No answer, the payment terminal still held up in front of him.

His heart rate quickened as he tried to muster some courage.

'I won't pay!' His voice sounded shaky, hesitant, afraid. As if the words that came out of his mouth were denoting the opposite of his intent not to pay. His tone suggested he would pay immediately with the tiniest amount of pressure.

The White Rabbit put his free hand into his back pocket and got out a laser pen and pointed it towards him. It was a very small pen, the type that produces a burning laser that can be fatal with long exposures, and in shorter bursts can burn and cause internal injuries. It's an illegal weapon used by gangs. One hand held out the payment terminal and the other held the pen. He had to choose one of them.

At this point his body started trembling. He had never been in such a situation before. Adrenaline coursed through his nerves and tensed his muscles. In all his boring life, back in the walled Capital, he had never experienced a rush like this. He felt like he might pass out at any moment.

His wrist monitor gave a high-pitched whistle indicating that his blood pressure was dangerously high. He reached with a shaky hand for the payment terminal and started inputting his details, but his eyes were blurred with tears. He put in the wrong information and couldn't figure out how to delete. He felt so broken; in all his life he had never felt this defeated. He was about to lose everything, and he couldn't do anything about it. Anger rose in his chest. He looked up to the White Rabbit and noticed that he'd put the laser pen back in his pocket. Maybe the Rabbit thought he was too pitiful to pose any threat. All he needed was a breath to be blown away. A stern look to wet his pants. Let's take this sucker's money and run. He is just a helpless insect.

The sunlight coming from the opening in the wall behind the White Rabbit was dazzling, and created a halo around his head that made him look somehow heavenly. There was a strong gust of humid air. Outside, the water suddenly seemed choppy due to the wind. The water stretched over vast distances between the ruins and derelict buildings that no longer had clearly defined features. Beneath the waters, thousands of pairs of feet had pounded the ground and thousands of voices had roared with anger. He had no hope in escaping. There was no way this would end without him dying. But doesn't the sacrificial lamb make one last kick? Without thinking, he lifted the terminal and, with all his strength, smashed it into the Rabbit's face. Blood spurted from the Rabbit's nose as he staggered backwards, stumbled on one of the boxes, and fell onto his back. He jumped on top of him and rained down blows on the Rabbit with the terminal still in his hand. The adrenaline was choking him and his wrist monitor was now screaming with beeps. But all he could hear was the sound of voices from outside. He was sitting on the Rabbit's chest and continuing to smash his face without stopping. The blood sprayed upwards like a fountain and splashed his face and eyes till all he could see was red everywhere. And still he didn't stop. He lost all sense of how long he'd been beating him for, and eventually it dawned on him that he'd killed the man. He collapsed to the floor, gasping for air. He lay on his back for a long time till he calmed down. He took off his shirt and wiped the blood from his face and eyes. It was as if he could see for the first time. His hearing slowly came back and the whistling of the wind and the sound of the waves breaking against the building replaced the echoing voices.

The body, with its face smashed in, was still there on the ground. He avoided looking at it. He was amazed at how easily it had come to pass. One minute he was sentenced to death and the next he was the master of his fate. What should he do now?

The ampoules! He searched the scattered boxes. They all had electronic circuits, storage devices and motherboards and other spare parts that he could not make out. He went over to the shelves. Old books and police outfits. Pipes and wires. Old statues and batteries. He looked for a long time but couldn't find any medicines. Were they the only two ampoules? He went over to the body while avoiding looking at the face. He put his hand in the pocket and was pricked by broken glass. He pulled out a bloody finger from the corpse's pocket. The two ampoules had been broken in the fight. Were they even genuine? He'd never know.

In any case it didn't matter. He still had his money and could try with someone else. He just needed to get out of here first. He walked over to the craft, crouched down by the opening in the wall. How do you get this thing to go? he wondered. He had never flown anything like this. The craft was sealed shut and had no door handles. It must have a biometric lock. He had no hope of opening it, let alone getting it to run, if he didn't know how to operate it.

The walls were solid and there was no exit. He went to the

opening and looked down. He reckoned he was on the fourth floor. There was no jumping from here as the water at the bottom was 1.5 metres deep at most. He got his phone out. Who could he call? There was no police service outside the walled areas, and nobody could get to him without using an illegal craft like the one he came in. Maybe if he could communicate with a friend over the internet, he could hire the services of another gang to get him out of there. The Black Raven or the Flaming Bear or whatever they called themselves.

Suddenly his phone notified him of an incoming internet call. The words 'The White Rabbit' appeared on the screen! How could that be? The corpse was still there on the ground. As he first suspected, the White Rabbit was the name of a gang and not an individual. The gang was calling. He answered the call and put the phone to his ear. He received a deluge of screams, insults and death threats. He looked around him and noticed the CCTV cameras installed on all the walls. The voice on the line told him they were coming to get him and his death was now guaranteed, then he advised him, if he wanted an easy death, to take his own life.

He let the phone drop to the ground. After thinking for a moment he'd won, here he was, waiting for a fate worse than death. He stood in the gap in the wall watching and waiting. The sun was setting. The wind had died down, and the voices fell silent. The sound of water spraying behind the approaching hovercraft was getting closer. It was the only sound he could hear.

Notes

1. Al-Maqrizi was a historian who documented a famine in Egypt during the rule of the Chaliph Al-Mustansir Billah between 1034-1096 AD.
2. A reference to the same famine during the Al-Mustansir Billah caliphate.

The Solitude of Prince Boudi

Ahmed Wael

Translated by Raphael Cohen

GENERATIONS OF PRINCE BOUDI's descendants grew up on the myth that a kingdom awaited them in Egypt. In Russia, Boudi's lineage would tell the tale of how their ancestor had only one purpose in life: to sire a dynasty to join him in a perpetual struggle for their rightful throne.

Over the course of more than 90 years, conceptions of this quest and its tactics changed, having included negotiations with the Egyptian army to found a constitutional monarchy, the writing of literature about the Boudian dispossession, and activism from exile in Russia. Then a certain Dimitri Boudi took a different approach to the legend.

Dimitri was well known for his non-violent struggle to liberate humanity from the cyber regime that controlled everywhere on Earth connected to the internet, and as part of his struggle Dimitri had set up alternative networks and currencies. Dimitri's life changed in 2111. The Arctic ice sheet grew back, in what represented a success for the global government's plan to refreeze the Arctic Ocean, which had been melting for decades. New seas, that had formed from the meltwater of the frozen ocean, froze again, as did old seas like the Caspian, Black, and Baltic. The global temperature dropped and the climate stabilised. Fears around global warming diminished. In spite of this, activists still had their doubts as to whether the climate would stabilise permanently and mobilised all the more militantly. Dimitri, however, did not get involved, preferring retirement in response to an inner calling: he was seized by the idea of becoming an artist. This artistic spirit confused him, bubbled up in his conscience, and drove him down an existential wormhole. He realised that years of his life had been wasted in activism and the time had come to relax.

Surrendering to this artistic spirit, Dimitri began to have weird dreams. He dreamt of his dead grandfather Boudi, who appeared as a young man fighting giant robots. In the tumult of battle, Boudi crooned a song unknown to Dimitri, who asked him what it was. 'It's Umm Kalthoum, Dimitri,' Boudi told him. '"All the people stood watching how we build the foundations of glory, I and Dimitri."'[1] The dream repeated night after night, and Dimitri tortured himself trying to understand it. He painstakingly unearthed the Umm Kalthoum song intended, but did not understand the significance of the change to the lyrics – instead of the grandfather building glory alone, he included Dimitri in the task. In his efforts to interpret the dream, he read his grandfather's novel *The Solitude of Prince Boudi*, but gained no insight. Then, inspired by the dream, he decided to visit his grandfather's birthplace, relying on the novel, which had become a masterpiece of Russian literature.

★

When, 96 years ago, the civil marriage between the Egyptian Abdel Rahman Shamashargi, nicknamed Boudi, and the Russian Katerina Dimitri Ivanova was registered at her country's embassy, the beautiful relationship growing in Dahab, Sinai, underwent developments that turned both their lives upside down. During the honeymoon, an airplane carrying Russian tourists exploded over the middle of the Sinai peninsula. Katerina got scared and felt that this sunlit paradise was not a safe place to live with Boudi. She decided to return post-haste to her country, but her husband, like most Egyptian men, took her decision as a hysterical one that could be overturned with humour. But Katerina's determination was greater than Boudi's sense of humour, and she did not respond to his efforts, insisting on putting their names down on her country's evacuation list, even though Boudi did not want to leave.

Katerina announced that she could never live in a place where people were blown up simply because their priority was to enjoy sea and sun far from enslavement to the new dictatorship ruling the world, one that relied on a complex synthesis between the digital state and capitalism. Katerina's way with words and her accurate description of the condition and future of humanity did not shake Boudi's will to stay in Egypt.

After days of giving him the silent treatment, Katerina told him that she could predict the future and foresaw the formation of a hegemonic world order. The future, as Katerina had imagined it long ago, would witness the coalescence of all regimes into a digital cloud that would rule humanity by means of artificial intelligence. She saw nation states shrinking into mere stops on a network of hypersonic hover-trains. She also predicted that human languages would revert to the pre-Babel period. Individual languages would disappear, replaced by a single programming language understood by all, be they human or robot.

Katerina predicted that not much time separated the world of nation states from the new world of the all-powerful digital cloud. Until that time ran out, she preferred to live in a strong entity not threatened by explosive devices. So she resolved to save herself and return to Russia.

When the Russian embassy called and told her to head to Cairo for evacuation to Russia, she gave Boudi one last chance. His response was a story that made little sense but, over the years, Katerina tried to fill in the gaps.

The story, which Boudi told all his foreign girlfriends holidaying in Dahab, began with his noble origins, how blue blood ran in his veins, even though his genealogy had never been officially recognised.

Boudi's family had served at the royal Abdeen Palace, where a royal crush took its course. The king fell in love with Camelia Shamashargi, and when she fell pregnant with the fruit of his royal crush, King Farouk turned her down and instructed a doctor to perform an abortion. But Camelia had the baby.

The family was expelled from the palace. Camelia was vilified and the story faded away with the new generation until Boudi revived it. Suspicions arose in his mind that his light-eyed, fair-haired and corpulent father was the spitting image of the king. When he aired these suspicions with his father, he kicked him out of the house, which only made Boudi cling to the story. He believed that King Farouk was his grandfather and that July 1952 represented the wrath of heaven at the king's denial of his son.

According to Boudi's story to Katerina – and to the women who came before her – the 1952 military coup only came about to serve the will of heaven in favour of the child that Farouk had denied. That child also bore a name akin to that of the crown prince and last king Ahmed Fouad for, in the story, Boudi's father was named Mohammed Fouad.

When the 2011 revolution erupted, Boudi tried to contact the army to propose a roadmap that the military leadership should follow:

the president to be exiled abroad and a caretaker administration formed;

the drawing up of a constitution founding a constitutional monarchy without an overweening president, in which the government would respect digitisation and liberties and lay the building blocks of good governance;

parliamentary elections free from fraud; and

Boudi being crowned king to the strains of trance music.

After intensive mediation by acquaintances, Boudi had a meeting with one of the army generals. The military commander treated him with derision, saying that the monarchy was dead and not about to be restored. Boudi did not leave the conference room, but raged that 59 years of army rule had only come about thanks to the birth of his father. The general grew annoyed but checked his anger, fearing that he might be dealing with the son of a clandestine leader from July 1952. He asked him politely, 'Who was your father, Mr Boudi?'

In response to the question, Boudi told his long story, causing the general to burst out laughing. He even called in other generals to listen. As Boudi repeated the story, the generals' laughter filled the room. In an effort to create a more serious atmosphere, a general tried to persuade Boudi to appeal to the people in Tahrir Square. The others joined forces with the serious general and suggested that Boudi appear on television, but ultimately he didn't feel comfortable doing so.

Boudi continued advocating his roadmap on Facebook but sensed that failure was inevitable. When the revolutionary camp started trolling him, he predicted the failure of the revolution itself, and the trolling only got worse. To escape it all, he moved to Dahab, where he worked organising scuba diving classes and trips to Abu Galoum.

Boudi always concluded his story to Katerina – and to the women who came before her – in the same way: 'This was until I met you, my angel! Being with you, I can forget all my losses: the throne, my father, and the revolution.'

Katerina was the only one who gave Boudi a chance to fulfil his khirati[2] dream. Not because she believed his story was true, but because of her panic over the plane crash. Thus Boudi won what every khirati aspires to: marriage to the woman in his sights followed by departure abroad.

When they went to Russia, Katerina, content with her own job, never made Boudi go out to work, but she did set him working on something else: his story. She prepped her husband very well and taught him Russian so that his story would have an audience in their town. Then, sensing similarities with the bloody end of the Romanovs, she made Boudi study the history of the Russian civil war – later called the Bolshevik Revolution. She focused on sources that made him visualise how the czar had been killed and how the blood of all those associated with him had been spilled; she told him about Rasputin. In this way, with Katerina's help, Boudi became thoroughly familiar with Russian literature.

Katerina did to the story what a sharp editor does to an ambitious text by a simple-minded writer. She made it clearer and more enjoyable where it had been pretentious and self-pitying, like most khiratis' stories. Thanks to Katerina, Boudi (or Abdel Rahman Shamashargi) took a more serious stance towards his story and wrote a novel inspired by its events that was published under the title *The Solitude of Prince Boudi*. Yet the source of what became literature remained an ever malleable story that Katerina told for educational purposes to her children, then her grandchildren and even her great-grandchildren. From the first time she heard it, she realised that the story was made up, but she gave its author a once-in-a-lifetime opportunity. Because of her long familiarity with the story, it became a means to many ends. She gave love a chance and turned a khirati into a global literary figure, a whiney child into a docile lamb, a nosey neighbour into a cherished friend, a drug addict of a son into an ambitious civil servant, and a rebellious grandson into a contemporary artist.

★

In his quest to understand his dream, Dimitri took the hypersonic hover-train. He did not know where his grandfather had been born, but he chose Dahab as the starting point. He had read about it in *The Solitude of Prince Boudi* and also heard about it in Katerina's stories. The place had become synonymous with love: Katerina's and Boudi's love; and, who knew, maybe love would find him there too. A love based on bodily communion, a love to blow the mind, a love forbidden by the robots that governed the enhanced systems of propagation.

THE SOLITUDE OF PRINCE BOUDI

Dimitri longed to find a love like the one that had changed his grandfather's life in Dahab 96 years before. He forgot his past as a digital activist and decided to purge his body of years of activism in the hope that the artistic spirit would give birth to a project or decode the symbolism of his dream.

In Dahab, he went diving and enjoyed catching fish before throwing them back in the sea. He searched for signs of his grandfather's story on the official Internet but could find nothing to confirm that it had ever happened. No mention of negotiations with the army; no trace of a roadmap towards constitutional monarchy; no information about the disavowed crown prince Mohammed Fouad. Switching to the dark web, and delving into a world free from the control of the cloud, he also failed to find the origins, or indeed any traces, of Prince Boudi's story. He did, however, pursue alternative interests such as drugs, trance music, and ideas of liberation from human enslavement to AI. He tried to throw himself into these activities by going to an underground party featuring the latest wave of trance music. He talked to one of the organisers, expecting her to be a khirati – the term his grandmother used for the people of Dahab – intending to rip him off. But his mistrust evaporated when she displayed interest in Prince Boudi. *Husna isn't a khirati*, he thought. She was against the system, used uncensored networks, and lived in a cave near the Blue Hole.

After going to the rave with her, Dimitri gave himself up to Husna and was enthusiastic about everything she suggested. He told her about his dream and asked her to interpret it. She advised him not to rely on the interpretation of dreams but to follow his heart. Now Dimitri's heart was urging him to love, to love Husna in Dahab and forget about his quest and his dream.

Dimitri walked behind Husna as they made their way towards the Blue Hole, hoping for any sign promising love and happiness.

Dimitri responded eagerly when Husna said, 'Let's do it.'

He prepared himself for her caresses and the taste of her lips, but Husna's invitation had another purpose. She pointed to where a path led down from the mountains to the sea, and told him to look at the waves beneath them: there, the devotees of Prince Boudi would swim and swear allegiance to his living descendant. Dimitri looked at the waves. Husna wrapped her left arm around his neck. In that moment, he expected love to overwhelm him, but instead Husna put a blade to his throat. She forced him to log on to the dark web and transfer all his real and crypto currency to her account. He complied and was then pushed into the sea.

As he overcame the breakers of the Blue Hole, Dimitri realised that Husna had used the story against him. She hadn't done so because she was super intelligent, but because she had found an easy target right in front of her who believed in the story of the dead khirati so much that it rendered him vulnerable to every possible form of trickery by a new khirati. It was as if the long-dead khirati had raised potential victims for future khiratis, who'd make use of bait that Katerina had overlooked despite all her efforts to develop the story.

The bait of the slippery khirati is love, which disarms and turns all into submissive souls who believe in the object of love even though they know a trick is being played. Those souls hold out the hope that true love will manifest itself once they get beyond the trick of the bait. When Dimitri reached the shore, one question troubled him: had Katerina warned them all about love or did she believe that love would only ever be fed by a trick in the form of a story?

Notes
1. 'Egypt Speaks About Herself', Umm Kalthoum, 1951.
2. A pejorative term for a hustler or tout who preys on tourists.

God Only Knows

Belal Fadl

Translated by Raphael Cormack

'WHAT DOES THE SHARIA rule about a man fucking himself in the arse?'

I found this question unpleasant, maybe even a little disgusting, but I can't say I was surprised to receive it. Over the past two years, I have encountered countless degenerate questions just like this one. Whenever I do, I always remember this piece of wisdom that my father handed down to me, and which he had heard in turn from *his* father, may he rest in peace: 'When you work in the fatwa business, you must be prepared for anything, no matter how filthy or decadent.'

My grandfather truly believed that muftis were, in essence, just like priests: obliged to listen to the most disgusting confessions from their congregants with quiet patience. He also told my father (who in turn told me): 'My boy, people open themselves up before you. They bare their souls to you in their letters and emails. Most people asking for a fatwa from you are not really looking for a specific religious ruling; they are looking for an opportunity to confess, to cleanse themselves, and to reassure themselves that the door to God's mercy has not yet been shut in their faces. It is our job to tolerate this, to understand it, to broaden our chests and to meet all the crap that comes our way. We ask God for His forgiveness, strength, and protection.'

I know that, compared to my father and grandfather, I am a nobody. I freely admit that. I was never given the honour that my father received to be appointed Grand Mufti of Egypt. Nor did I reach the heights that my grandfather did when he was made head of the Fatwa Committee in the Academy of Islamic Studies at al-Azhar. He, too, would have become Sheikh of al-Azhar, had it not been for the controversy that followed his fatwa permitting the use of VAR technology in people's bedrooms in order to resolve marital disputes. This fatwa made him the subject of considerable scorn and mockery when he was alive. It was only after his death that people began to appreciate its value. When the judges started following this fatwa, they discovered that many couples suddenly began to resolve their problems themselves instead of dragging them in front of the court, which would simply examine the 'tapes', determine which party was lying, punish them appropriately, and force them to pay tens of thousands of pounds in legal expenses.

My grandfather (unlike my father) did not write any detailed memoirs of his long career in the Academy of Islamic Studies and the Fatwa Committee. But he did pass on many stories to my father about our family's journey through the profession of mufti – the person who issues fatwas. My father's voice would quaver when he talked about our family's work and he would declare, referencing the words of the Quran, that if such a hard job 'was offered to the heavens, the earth, and the mountains, they would refuse.' After a little time, though, I came to realise that he was wrong: no one would refuse a job that contained all the entertaining little nuggets which reached my desk every day in fatwa requests. Perhaps this perk is what pushed so many of my predecessors to follow the calling.

The first was my great-great-grandfather, who worked as an assistant in the National Fatwa Institute when it was established in 1895. He had a bright future ahead of him until he was forced to resign after he refused to permit the Khedive Abbas Hilmi II to kill his ex-wife Djavidan, who had demanded a divorce and gone to become a singer in Berlin. He told the Khedive that he should not have chosen 'green manure' for a wife – 'a beautiful woman of bad origin' – as the Prophet had warned.

This ancestor of mine – who paid a heavy price for these words – was the first and last rebellious mufti in my family. Everyone who came after him learned his lesson (even if he did not). They knew that a mufti, without a ruler to protect and support him, is always vulnerable and liable to attack: As the Hadith says, 'Whoever God does not restrain by the Quran, He restrains by the ruler.' Or, as the old proverb goes, 'Fear is better than mercy.' My ancestors' experiences, as recorded by my father, have confirmed the truth of these words.

I have learned from them that, although public anger at unpopular fatwas can be bad, it passes (no matter how intense it is at first); the anger of a ruler has a deadlier sting. Popular anger is changeable; when the heavy weight of reality reveals the benefits of a fatwa they had previously rejected, they might then accept it. The ruler's anger, on the other hand, arrives swiftly and leaves no possibility for redress or appeal. I have learned the wisdom of my forefathers well. Of course, a mufti must, above all, fear the wrath of God, who will judge him at the end if he panders to the whims of the people and issues fatwas he does not believe in. But after the Lord, he should fear the wrath of the powerful, who can easily remove him from his position and deprive the people of his knowledge and learning.

So, if you find that you are issuing fatwas which the ruler does not understand and which are hard to adopt or defend, you must do all you can to communicate their benefits to them. You soon realise that prudence is a more important quality for a mufti than boldness. Producing a carefully submitted fatwa – or, if you prefer, a carefully submissive fatwa – will help bring you closer to the faithful and, in turn, bring the faithful closer to their Lord.

When I was born in 2052, my father was at the peak of his fame. He had just issued his historic fatwa forbidding fasting during the day for Ramadan if the temperature exceeded 50 degrees centigrade – on the basis that almighty God did not approve of casting souls into oblivion in this way. But this fatwa would never have been accepted in the hearts of millions, had my father not also added the stipulation that those obliged to fast should do so for a full month in the winter (the precise dates to be decided by the ruler and his advisors) to make up for their lack of fasting in the summer.

Despite this, the fatwa still met with violent resistance from many at first. But as mortality rates climbed, this resistance fell away, particularly after the long power cuts that came frequently as the electricity grid failed to cope with the deadly temperature rises. It was thanks to this fatwa, which saved millions of lives, that my father rose from an ordinary teacher at al-Azhar to head of Islamic Studies at age 32. Five years later he became the youngest Grand Mufti in Egyptian history. My father always told me that his decision to add his small appendix about fasting in winter had saved him from the terrible fate which had befallen the two previous muftis. I soon learned that if I ever published a fatwa declaring anything Halal or Haram, I should always append several religiously sanctioned alternatives to the fatwa that people could choose from. Of course, I know that people ask for fatwas so they don't have to think too much about the ins and outs of the issue, not to give themselves another headache. But I need to protect myself.

Some jealous people have criticised me for sitting on the

fence too much; they point out that my father's wisdom did not prevent him from taking some difficult and controversial positions. By trying not to annoy anyone, I ended up annoying them more. Now, I am in my last year before retirement. Of course, I *was* hoping that everyone would say, after my journey came to an end, that Shaykh Shihab al-Din Draz Gad al-Haq al-Batanuni had surpassed both his grandfather and his father in knowledge, skill, and influence on people's lives. But they had better luck than me. People in my father's and grandfather's era had a different relationship to fatwas than we have now. After the radical changes that swept the country in the 21st century, fatwas went from being a matter of personal choice – something to reassure confused people – to being an important way to deal with a world that was undergoing several unprecedented crises. Fatwas in this period became more like on-the-spot legal rulings, which the government enforced with an iron fist, in an attempt to preserve the social contract.

But in my time, Lord only knows, fatwas have become little more than logic games, just like they were in the time of the Abbasid caliphate when people lived in comfort and ease. People compete with each other to pose stupid questions designed to test the mental skills (and sometimes the patience) of the muftis or just to pass their own time. Sometimes I feel that I have been turned into a talisman instead of a person. People claim to come to me for my opinion but really they are just seeking my blessing – a seal of approval for a decision that they have already made. In this debased environment, questions about people fucking themselves in the arse are actually better than the other shitty questions I get asked every day.

Perhaps this is because the question about arse-fucking is not entirely divorced from reality. The request for this fatwa originally came after the invention, two years ago in Holland, of a hideous device that somehow fulfilled the sick desires of those who wanted to have sex with themselves – I did not ask about the details of how it worked at the time, following the words of the Almighty, 'Do not ask about things which, if they are revealed, will cause you harm.' But now that I have to issue a fatwa about it, I am forced to look into its workings. The person seeking the fatwa even asked if this machine might be permissible and if it might be consistent with older fatwas which permitted masturbation as an alternative to forbidden sexual intercourse. He seemed very pleased with himself when he argued that there was very little fundamental difference between the hand and the anus, in the goal of keeping people away from fornication. Lord have mercy.

The world keeps changing; sometimes it changes for the worse and sometimes for the better, but it always changes. If we are wise, we must always keep the principles of the Sharia that we serve in mind. We should accept these changes to our reality without falling into self-pity. I have no problem spending my time answering tens of stupid or degenerate questions every day. It weighs on my soul but it is better than being the target of an assassination attempt, after which I might lose the use of my legs and spend the rest of my life going to the toilet with the help of a robot, as happened to my grandfather when he issued a fatwa permitting abortion in 2045. The extremists showed him no mercy on account of his old age nor his long service to his religion. If only they had contented themselves with calling for his blood from the pulpits of their mosques, questioning his faith, and abusing him. But they also decided to blow up his car where, if the grace of God had not saved him, he would have died.

That explosion did not only take his legs; it also took away his calm composure and wide smile that never failed to cheer up his friends. He died a grieving man. If he had lived just five years longer, he would have seen society change and realise that his fatwa actually protected them when a destructive famine came to Egypt after the Nile Valley experienced a true drought for the first time in its history – something no one believed could ever really happen. Then, people were not just considering whether to kill their foetuses or not; they were thinking about which of their living children they had to kill to save the others.

The world became very different after this. In the 2070s, when my father issued his fatwa permitting same sex marriage, every Islamic country adopted it and no religious scholars had any issues with it. This was not because of his skills of persuasion; reality convinced everyone to accept it – even rejoice in it. This fatwa put an end to the destruction of households and brought together families that had been torn apart by estrangements and disownings. Just 30 years previously, people had been convinced that, if a fatwa like this were ever issued, it would be due to pressure from Western countries and the diversity policies of international companies, who would make accepting homosexuality a condition of doing business with anyone in the world.

Reality proved that everything people had said or written in the olden days about 'the gay lobby', which they claimed was more powerful than the 'Zionist lobby', was (as usual) an exaggeration. What really gave hundreds of thousands of people a more tolerant attitude towards their gay children and siblings was the constant struggle to stay alive and not die of thirst, suffocate in the deadly heat, or get killed by one of the criminal gangs that did not distinguish between people with homosexual and heterosexual desires. In time, people came to realise that it was better for people to be openly gay and spare everyone the problems that came when people tried to conceal their sexual identity. The whole fuss about sexual orientation disappeared. Instead of cursing those who had talked about gay marriage, people began to mock anyone who was attached to the concept of marriage at all.

All of these developments were important, but they were not enough for my father to issue his fatwa. The necessary precondition for that came with a military coup in the 2060s by a group known as the 'Free Queers', whose first act was to declare an end to the discrimination against gay people that had been practiced in the military since its establishment. Egypt was in such a state of economic and social turmoil that no one paid much attention to this new group in charge of the country, with its provocative name, which had been chosen as a play on the 'Free Officers' of the 1950s, in revenge for the torture and oppression that they and the gay people who came before them had suffered in Egypt. A meme spread like wildfire through the country, encapsulating popular opinion about this new era and its new leaders: 'At least they are fucking each other instead of fucking us.'

As usual, enthusiasm for this new age was short lived. Everyone soon discovered that their problems were too deep to be solved by the religion or sexual orientation of their leaders. The 'Free Queers' were overthrown after bloody battles with various other organisations all with the word 'Free' in their names. Fortunately for Egyptians, none of these groups were strong enough to definitively triumph over their competitors. The bloody struggle ended with a comprehensive political agreement, after which the military establishment left power forever, having definitively proven itself incapable of solving any of the crises that had faced it over the 120 years it had been in power. Were it not for all of this, my father would never have been able to issue his fatwa which ended debate on homosexuality forever – or, to be a little more realistic, ended debate on it for a while.

'The past always returns.' Ever since I can remember, I have heard my father repeat this phrase, which I rather liked. When I was younger, I thought it was one of the sayings of the Prophet or His companions, but when I grew up, I discovered that it was actually the title of an old soap opera. I would have watched it if my father hadn't described it as 'a load of rubbish' – an opinion that he had inherited from his own father, who had also taught him the phrase. His father had told him that all the millions of years of human history could be summed up in these words. People have an uncanny ability to repeat their mistakes, to relive their old sorrows and old battles, to pour old piss into new pots, if you will.

My grandfather always refused calls to get rid of the old books of jurisprudence, with their strange and unusual fatwas. He thought that it was important for anyone issuing fatwas to study these old texts, not just as a mental exercise to learn from the experiences of those who had come before him, but also to learn how the great muftis through the years took on the serious responsibility of solving people's problems and protecting them from corruption, even if they did it in strange ways. They knew the importance of the juridical principle: 'Wherever you find a benefit for humanity, you are turning towards God.' Take, for example, the old view that a foetus could stay inside the mother for three of four years before birth. They did not say this because they were stupid or crazy. They were rational. They did not want warriors returning from years away at battle to kill their wives who had given birth in their absence because they had besmirched their honour.

Of course, my grandfather never imagined that the fatwas which had so angered people in his day, would become the subject of research in future times. People asked for a ruling on cryogenic freezing technologies, which could freeze people's loved ones so they could stay with them after death. A huge controversy erupted over the permissibility of sexual intercourse with a frozen wife, if the husband was unable to love anyone else. On another occasion, a whole meeting of the Organisation of Islamic Cooperation was taken up with finding a way to make eating pork Islamically permissible after a rare virus wiped out all other types of livestock on the planet, leaving the pig as the only source of protein for Muslims. Pork became the latest forbidden thing that a necessity forced Muslims to permit. Before this, medical advances had eliminated all of the negative effects that alcohol had on those who drank it. So, as far as the Sharia was concerned, it became just another drink; though doctors still warned about its effects on people with obesity – this remains the only physical disease for which no cure has been found, after science discovered ways to eradicate cancer, heart disease, diabetes, and high blood pressure. We are still waiting, though, for a cure for depression, whose deadly effects still claim thousands of victims every day around the world, especially after the fatwa which made it permissible to kill a depressed person if they are causing harm to those around them. All these fatwas may always be brought into question again, doubted, or rejected, as many fatwas before them have been.

When my beloved father died ten years ago, one of his transgender students became Sheikh of al-Azhar and I do not think anyone who occupied this position has ever been loved as much as he was. God had given him an incredible ability to communicate with people and open their hearts. Many responded to his calls to return to the tenets of old-fashioned morality, in particular chastity of the tongue. This was a virtue which had been abandoned in the previous decades, after a fatwa had been issued in the 2020s making it permissible to turn a blind eye to obscene language as a way to help people relieve the pressures of the deteriorating social and economic situation. It was justified on the basis that God allows 'those who have been wronged' to say bad things. This fatwa helped reduce the number of spouses who were killed, the random shootings, and violence on public transport which were common at the time.

Once the social and economic conditions improved, after Egypt's population had halved due to famine, disease, and civil war, people still didn't stop using foul language, even when it could no longer be justified as a way to let off steam; it had rather simply become an integral part of their lives. In recent years, millions have answered the Sheikh of al-Azhar's call to resist and reject foul language, putting an end to the illusion that anything lasts forever. He was also extremely wise in dealing with negative reactions to him, especially to the insults he received from people who were attached to swearing and were angry at him for trying to take that away. He jokingly read out the things they said to him on his daily television programme 'Spiritual Talk', which for years had been the most popular and influential show in the whole country.

I am sure that what happened with foul language will happen to many other things that my father, grandfather, and those who preceded them thought would last forever. This is why I have schooled myself in the art of what some call 'sitting on the fence', but what I prefer to call (in football terminology) being more responsive in the midfield. I know that flexibility and the ability to adapt to a changing reality are the two strongest weapons that people like me, who live by their intellects and their tongues, can rely on in rapidly changing times like these. I ask God almighty that I not become seduced by my own mind and quick tongue and think that my intelligence shields me from any responsibility to God and his difficult tests. Only those who please the Almighty will pass through these travails, reach happiness on earth and gain the rewards of the hereafter. O kind and gentle Lord, who hears the prayers of the righteous, count me among their number.

Unicorn2512

Nora Nagi

Translated by Mayada Ibrahim

UNICORN2512 DECIDED TO WRITE a story.

She had been thinking about it for 30 years, but had never taken any concrete steps. Maybe it was because, ever since her mother died, smiling at her with an expression of pity on her face, she had never quite been able to organise her thoughts. Her mother's expression robbed her of sleep. It snuck into her field of vision every time she tried to watch a film or think up a new status or try a new app. She couldn't focus. It haunted her even as she wandered the colourful streets or spent time with her friends at the clubhouse.

The smile grew and grew until it took over her entire vision, as bright as the advertisements that covered the metaverse sky before her eyes, which she saw clearly despite her limited eyesight. She couldn't see or walk or swallow or touch or hear very well, but it was only when she decided to write a story that she remembered that she had a body, for the first time in years. She held her hand in front of her face to make sure it was there, but she didn't recognise it. She lifted her other hand, looked down at her chest and stomach, ran her fingers along her legs and pulled the little hairs growing on them. She didn't feel anything and wondered whether she was someone else – a person inside another person, or a thing inside a person, like something out of the old horror films she watched on an app and scoffed at. She imagined her mother transforming into a creature that snuck inside her; a little monster that placed its tentacles on her skin and slid into a hole in her face to take control of her.

Why did her mother smile at her like that? What did her smile mean? She never stopped wondering, so she decided to write a story.

But how could she tell a story without a voice?

Unicorn2512 couldn't remember the last time she used her voice. It could have been the day her mother died, 30 years prior. She had been wandering the streets of the metaverse, other loners walking alongside her, when she received a message from the House of Noncompliance, telling her to return to the other world to see her mother before she passed. The message had appeared beside her quite suddenly, then it was replaced by a megaphone that projected a frigid voice speaking in English, the only language still permitted globally: 'Before she dies.'

The voice added that her mother requested to see her and urged her to hurry, since the other world – the real one perhaps, or the one that once was real – still depended on time, while time in the metaverse was illusory. She was instructed to remove the mask attached to her face in order to regain the sensation in her limbs and in the rest of her neglected body. She was to find something to wear and use the mirror abandoned in the corner of her room, walk onto the empty street, and make her way to the House of Noncompliance, built on land that had once been a park. She was to regain her voice so that she could say goodbye to her mother.

She stood in front of the bed where her mother lay in the

House of Noncompliance and said goodbye. The building would later turn into a pitch-black collective grave when the last of the dissenters died. Her mother did not speak, even though she sacrificed everything for speaking. She looked at Unicorn2512 – her fifty-something-year-old daughter who had lost her senses – with pity in her eyes. She smiled. Then she died.

When Unicorn2512 returned to her room, she let her mother's belongings, which she'd been handed upon leaving the building, fall to the ground. She was about to put the mask and gloves back on, but she hesitated and just lay for a while on the bed, not in a hurry to get back to her home in the metaverse, even though it was a beautiful villa that she had spent years in artificial labour to save up for. It never really felt like it belonged to her. People were always barging in and she had no say in the matter. They were usually on some kind of mission – harvesting diamonds or starting friendships or exchanging goods.

There was no such thing as privacy in the metaverse. Or rather, Unicorn2512 would say that there was no privacy in the life she knew. It wasn't just messages that appeared out of the blue; anyone could break into your home at any time – in the bathroom or the bedroom, while you're having sex or watching a film or trying to cry (which, in the virtual world, looks like two waterfalls frozen by each eye). Maybe that was why her mother refused to stay, even though staying would have meant she lived indefinitely. Unicorn2512 would have signed the life-after-death agreement and split her savings with her, and paid the 2,000 diamonds it cost to house her mother's spirit on an app. She could have remained embodied. Together they could have taken walks, shopped in supermarkets, reorganised their closets, and met friends at the clubhouse. Perhaps then she wouldn't have looked at her with so much pity on her final day. She would have disappeared for a moment then reappeared again next to Unicorn2512. But her mother refused. She preferred to be moved to the House of Noncompliance with those who said no to the new world and it was there she remained, in the shadows, depleting her body, wearing old clothes that had long stopped being manufactured, watching an endless stream of inanity on the enormous television hanging on a wall. Maybe she played chess or backgammon with the last surviving generation of the old world.

How would Unicorn2512 write a story without language?

Her mother was a writer. Unicorn2512 remembered that clearly. She used to sit next to her on the bed while she typed on her laptop. She wrote then paused to answer her questions. Sometimes she erupted and told her to leave the room. Sometimes she kissed her and apologised for being distant. Sometimes she disappeared for days because of work, leaving her with her grandmother, who died before the old world ended. Sometimes she took her along to boring meetings in bookshops and stuffy, dusty rooms. But she always made sure that they took walks together. She held her hand and they walked without talking. She was always absent-minded, but she never smiled at her pityingly.

Unicorn2512 only inherited a small suitcase. It didn't contain much. A few books with a photo of her mother on each of them. Yellowing papers. Two old jackets. A plastic container with several colourful earrings, a handheld fan, a dried-out pen, a purse with faded pieces of paper. She unfolded one and found a drawing of a red heart and the first letter of her real name in English and Arabic next to the first letter of her mother's name.

She remembered the day she drew that picture when she was a child. Her name was coming back to her. It started with an F in English, and ف in Arabic, a dead language. The sounds were coming back to her in both languages. In Arabic, it was pronounced like a gentle breath, the top teeth softly touching the lower lip. In English, it was pronounced with a slight constriction in the throat that abates as the upper teeth touch the lower lip, remaining trapped in the space between the tongue and the roof of the mouth, like inedible food she is unsure whether to swallow or spit out.

She leafed through one of the novels. The letters made sense to her and she was able to make out her name on the first page of each novel. She discovered that language did not simply die, as they tried to convince everyone in the metaverse. It was not lost to her. Just as her voice was not lost to her; she regained it when saying goodbye to her mother. At that moment, she decided to re-establish her relationship with language and read every word ever written by this woman who left smiling.

Thirty years later, Unicorn2512 looked at the reams of papers scattered around her and her body shivered.

News reached her in the morning that the last of the dissenters had died at 110 years old. There were none left. The news was announced with a hint of relief. Unicorn2512 could sense it despite the tinny voice of the news presenter. She knew the dissenters were a burden on the state, which still performed its duties from the new capital city – 80 years old but still somehow considered new. Even though the establishment of a new capital city in the metaverse had been a source of continuous debate for years, no one dared to make any demands or objections outright. The government paid a huge sum of money to the company Meta, but received nothing in return. Building a virtual capital city does take time, as much time as a real capital city. Perhaps Meta was working on algorithms capable of creating an exact clone of the capital, including its walls and buildings and all the flyovers that lead to it – even though none of that was necessary. Concerns were raised about the potential disclosure of the governor's identity. With his name readily accessible on the web, anyone could storm his palace at any time. Should he choose, instead, to enter a confidentiality agreement, he would have to disappear for some time while the move was in process. And this killed him; so keen was he on broadcasting his speeches in Egypt's metaverse on a daily basis, and using the latest animation technology to display his image on its streets. But these are just speculations that young people exchanged on street corners and in front of brightly lit cafés. They laughed, which in the metaverse looked like holding their hands to their mouths, bearing shiny teeth. Some say that the governor himself was just an avatar. Because even with the recent advancements in medicine, the eradication of contaminants, the prevalence of life-extending treatments to maintain population numbers after they had fallen to a quarter due to the Corona pandemic in 2020, the Great War in 2040, the subsequent drop in the birth rate and the total suspension of all fertility treatments – it still was not plausible for him to look the same age for a hundred years.

The government ensured that every real city had a counterpart in the metaverse, and that all its inhabitants were also its inhabitants in the metaverse. But it changed the layout of the streets. It erased oceans and lakes and the Nile, which had run dry anyway, in favour of intersecting streets, like a chess board. It also eliminated desert, agricultural, and international highways, as well as roads connecting provinces, because they were no longer useful. It was enough to click on someone's name to hop into their home or wherever they happen to be. Public squares were also eliminated because a virtual revolution in the metaverse was just as terrifying as a real revolution in a real square, even a static square protected by crumbling rams.

Unicorn2512 lived in the city of Tanta, which still held on to its character: the many cafés and restaurants, its inhabitants' love of food, their sweet tooth, and their inclination towards the arts. In Tanta, young people sat on street corners and the sidewalks of cafés, carrying strange-looking instruments. With the press of a button, they became virtuosic musicians, and just as easily they switched to drawing, football, singing, dancing…

How did the government manage to provide monthly provisions? Who farmed and who manufactured? Who turned food into compacted powder, who packaged and who distributed? She didn't know the answers. She didn't even ask the questions through all these years. She just worked, changing her virtual job every two months, or whenever she felt like it. A fashion designer, a chef, a supermarket clerk, a dentist, a teacher. She received her salary in pink diamonds. She paid her taxes and shopped to her heart's content.

A distant memory flickered. When she was four, her mother had taken her someplace beautiful. She and a few other children were role-playing. She put out a fire and distributed mail and made yoghurt and baked pizza. She recalled the sound of her laugh and the way her mother looked when she took photos of her using her phone, when people still carried phones and took photos.

Unicorn2512 considered writing a story about her own life.

As one of few people still alive to have known the other life, she believed that the metaverse's existence has come to prove that time had been standing still for the final hundred years, and also to prove that her generation had been plagued by forgetfulness since birth. But she hadn't used her voice in 30 years, and that made her a bad protagonist by any measure, besides the fact that she was old, 80 years old, and looked like a skeleton. If it were up to her, if she were actually a good storyteller, she would choose a different protagonist, like her mother, or one of the undertakers who were content to remain and dispose of the decomposing bodies, without a metaverse identity, without provisions or any sense of security. They were fertile material. They held on to their faith after it had been abolished from the world. They were satisfied providing salvation to those who died alone in their tiny rooms.

All homes had turned into metre-by-metre rooms, with each person sitting in front of a screen that covered a wall. People died and their rooms became graves. They were left surrounded by their belongings, their garbage, and boxes of provisions and ridiculous accessories bought from metaverse stores that could only be used in the metaverse, stuffed in the small space between the bed and the screen, piled up in front of the door. At some point, the assumption that graves had to be in the ground, and graveyards located on the outskirts of the city was called into question. Homes could now be graveyards too where the living lived among the dead. Because no one died completely, neither in reality nor virtually.

She thought up a story whose protagonist was one of the workers who had the right to live in both worlds. During the day, he and others like him pretended to work to appease the masters in the distant capital city. At night, they returned to the virtual world to unburden their eyes, hearts, and minds from the weight of reality. Their senses had not wasted away because they still had to urge their bodies to work every day. These were the real heroes. As for her, she was just an old woman by the old world's standards, even though she was still in her twenties in the metaverse.

She realised that the reason she had forgotten what her body looked and felt like, was that she no longer feared passing away, disintegrating, disappearing. She knew that the world would turn black and then she would regain consciousness and continue her life in a natural way, in the world she had lived in for most of her life. She wouldn't even know that she had died until she discovered that she no longer needed to leave her little room.

Since her mother had died, she had only left her room a handful of times. If it were up to her, she wouldn't leave at all, but the government forced everyone to renew their IDs in person every six months. It was a new protocol they introduced ten years ago when they noticed that the number of undertakers had dropped. The undertakers had become isolated and stopped reproducing, which meant that people were dying and decomposing without their deaths being recorded. The government was forgiving when it came to neglecting to record the occasional natural birth, but with death, they were not so forgiving.

It never occurred to her to volunteer to mate or to donate her eggs. She enjoyed having sex via dating apps. It satisfied her for days before she thought about repeating the experience, much like eating or drinking or flying or running or swimming or jumping or feeling fear or joy. Pure simulated emotion guaranteed that everyone could remain in their new world. They never needed to go back. Even her maternal impulses were satisfied for a while by having an artificial baby, though he quickly grew tiresome. The baby remained the same age, the same size. She exchanged him with a cat, then a penguin, then a pink bear, then a green dinosaur that breathed fire and flew, carrying her on its back. The women who volunteered to mate were heroes. Theirs were stories that could have been written had writing – or language, or emotion, or thought – not come to an end.

But all her thoughts changed when she decided that the moment to write a story had come.

The idea came to her as she went to grab her blue jacket from the closet. She happened to catch a glimpse of her room in the mirror: small, dusty, messy, papers scattered everywhere. She saw her attempts at writing using pens she bought from antique shops and had shipped to her along with the provisions. She saw her emaciated body and the wrinkles on her face. It dawned on her that she didn't have long left. She was going to die that day. The image of her thin body dying in the middle of that mess unleashed a panic inside her. It brought back the ghost of her mother's smile.

Unicorn2512's body shivered. For the first time, she was afraid of leaving. She knew that transforming into a pure avatar meant that she could remain alive, though she wouldn't breathe the way she was breathing in that moment, the stagnant air carrying a strange smell she was noticing for the first time. She wouldn't bat her eyelids. She wouldn't place her hands on her face. She wouldn't use the bathroom or take a shower or eat the tasteless pureed food. More importantly, she wouldn't write her story. She wouldn't read it at the next clubhouse as she planned, explaining to herself in front of others why her mother looked at her pityingly before she died, which meant she would never find the answer to her question. She would die and come back to life and she would forget everything. The questions that preoccupied her no longer would once she transformed into pure avatar, but she also wouldn't be at ease.

Unicorn2512 decided to sit down to write immediately, to describe her mother's smile in detail, to recount all the memories she shared with her, to recall every letter of her name in Arabic. She would finally cut language open. She would speak it aloud as if inventing it anew. She didn't know many words, so she would use AI to translate her thoughts into words. The translation would be written in the air before her. She would read it aloud on the streets of the metaverse, and in her room. People in neighbouring rooms would hear her. Thus her mission would be complete. Her mother's pitying smile would disappear. It would be replaced with a smile that would be serene. She would die again the moment Unicorn2512 died. They would both be at peace.

Unicorn2512 put down the final word. She wrote 'peace', added a full stop, and was seized with joy. She felt like she was walking on clouds. The text was complete. It was a real work, a new creation, a being, like a child that would not remain an infant forever. She put on her mask and gloves and left the house, heading to a place she used to love, the place that had once been occupied by a giant clock. The clock had been removed and the area was turned from a square into an ordinary road. She stood exactly in the middle and read.

Unicorn2512 didn't notice when her voice began to fade.

In the real world, where the clock once stood, she also stood still. Meanwhile, in the virtual world, her body grew, ran, leapt. The other world's features changed every few minutes. Around her, in both worlds, people meandered in silence, listening without understanding, trying to read the English translation in the metaverse, or recalling a word or two in Arabic from a distant past. She heard mumbling voices identifying words. She heard laughs and applause and cheers to keep going. Before she could resume, her lips moved soundlessly and she could no longer hear anything. Her vision started to blur.

She lifted her hand to her face and saw that she was vibrating and fading. She lifted her eyes to the crowd around her. They were looking at her with curiosity that was turning into panic. They were witnessing a rare instance of the supervisor punishing the citizen. She was disappearing bit by bit. A message, in red, flew to her side, telling her that she was violating the laws of the metaverse and the government, and that her punishment, a total ban, was in effect immediately.

Unicorn2512 disappeared within seconds. Even her life-after-death agreement was void. She no longer was. All because someone far away who watched everything was afraid. He was afraid of words that were no longer being used. Words like death, master, grave, language. So he decided to ban her. But the people around her remained where they were. They circled the place where she had stood and read. They wanted to hear the end of the story. Some tried to use their own voices and succeeded. They began to discover what it meant to speak. Some even managed to utter whole words. It was a strange moment. It resembled the moment of the pitying mother's smile, capable of changing the world, even though, in reality, it was nothing.

Days later, a curious child, who knew who Unicorn2512

was and which room she occupied, wanted to find out how the story ended. He knocked on the door for hours on end but she didn't answer. He walked the streets of the metaverse asking for help. He did so using his voice and quickly attracted attention. He was led out of the metaverse to Unicorn2512's door, and when they broke the door down, they found her dead, among reams of papers, smiling peacefully, and for the first time, they grieved.

The thought of leaving her where she was, in that room, struck them as odd. For the first time, they felt that the dead and living ought to be apart, not out of fear, but out of some kind of reverence. They didn't want to be reminded of their falseness. No, Unicorn2512 had to be moved elsewhere. Without uttering a word, they carried her to the street where she had read her story. They surrounded her with items found scattered around: wooden frames, bags full of unknown objects, decaying tree branches, pieces of white marble, old mirrors, her papers, pens, and blue jacket. They set out to read to her. Each person chose a word. Every day more people joined, and continued to read, copying new sentences, adding more papers. By the time they had laid down the last paper, with her real name printed on top, which they copied from her mother's novels, her body had vanished. The street in the metaverse and in the real world turned suddenly into a public square.

Mama

Camellia Hussein

Translated by Basma Ghalayini

I SAW MYSELF SURROUNDED by darkness, drowning in a thick, sticky substance. I opened my mouth to scream, and only the words 'Mama, Mama' escaped. Why did I call for Mama? I'm old and Mama passed away years ago.

I saw my arms and legs flailing about in all directions, just before I hit a wall – firm, but breakable. All it took was a gentle push with my palm, and it burst like a boil. I was flung backwards onto the ground, cushioned by the viscous liquid surrounding me.

I saw myself in a vast forest, surrounded by countless trees. I was lying on the ground next to a huge tree, its trunk maybe two metres in diameter. In its enormous trunk, I could see dozens of gashes, each covered with what looked like a primitive fabric made of plant fibres. One of them was torn and exuding a glutinous fluid. This is where I had come out.

I saw myself getting up and tearing at the fabric covering one of the incisions. While a tiny child's palm stretched out from the inside, I reached out my hand, and it clung to my finger and started calling 'Mama! Mama!' I tried to pull the baby out, but I couldn't, it was heavy and clung on tight. It started pulling me into the tree. I tried to get away from it while also shouting 'Mama! Mama!' The delicate palm gripped tighter, mewling, 'Mama! Mama!'

The infant's innocent voice started to merge with the loud, collective chants of 'Mama... Mama... Egypt is Mama.' I opened my eyes and got out of bed. I looked over at the balcony, whose windows I had forgotten to close, muttering, 'Fuck Mama.'

As I prepared my coffee in the kitchen and filled a jug of water for my plants, the tree and its crevices faded from my thoughts. I inserted a pair of earplugs to block out the incessant chanting, then picked up the jug and coffee, and headed to the balcony.

'Good morning,' I said to the plants, and started reviewing the smart watering console attached to each pot: 30mm for the small one, and 250mm for the next one. As for the cactus, its vase flashed that he could wait another two days. I continued to water the rest of the plants on the balcony railing and the ones hanging on the wall.

I gazed at the collection of smart pots, with their blinking consoles that told me everything; the amount of water needed, the degree of fertilisation, the condition of the roots, and the acidity of the soil. I thought of my first plant; it was in an ordinary container, and I used to water it every morning and evening so it never got thirsty. But the leaves gradually turned yellow and fell. I watered it more, thinking it needed more, not realising that the roots below were rotting, and that overwatering was causing them to drown. Until the plant was reduced to a lonely, naked twig sticking out of the soil.

I looked down at the street: lines of honourable citizens stretched as far as the eye could see, immaculate rows of men and women with similar features wearing identical clothes. I could hear their chants even through my earplugs.

I sat down on the floor, with my back to the solid balcony wall to escape the sight. I reached into my toolbox and took out a piece of cotton wool, dipped it in water, and picked up my oldest plant. I wiped its soft bright green leaves, one after another. This little one was the strongest, it had fought against all odds. I remembered how its little buds appeared after I had fixed its irrigation, its leaves slowly covering the single bare twig until it became the most beautiful of all my plants.

'Mama... Mama... Egypt is Mama... Bring the children to Mama.' I could still hear the chanting; I pressed my palms to the earplugs to no avail. I thought of my poor plants, and how I couldn't protect them at all from this noise. My fingers felt the green branches and leaves, and patted the wet silt. I wondered if at least this silt could protect the roots from the cacophony. I stroked the surface of the soil gently with my fingertips, careful not to disturb it, remembering how I dug it with my bare fingers for the first time.

I could still recall the muffled thud of him falling out of my body onto the bathroom floor. He didn't fall into the toilet like I was expecting. Suddenly, he was in front of me on the cold floor, covered in blood.

He was the size of a sesame seed when first I knew he was there, and the size of a grape when I decided to get rid of him. When I bent down that day to look at him, he was the size of a plum, with a small head, two arms, and two feet. I sat next to him on the cold ground, picked him up with my fingertips, and placed him on my palm. I brought him close to my face to contemplate him after I gently wiped the blood off his face, mindful not to squash him. With a little imagination, I knew that these features would have grown into a copy of mine.

I could see his internal organs through his translucent body, and in the middle of his chest was a clear point. Is this his heart? I brought him close to my ear, but I didn't hear anything. I remember feeling horrified; maybe his heart is still beating, and I can't hear him. What am I doing? Should I try to put him back in my body? What if he dies before I can get him back in? Worse still, what if I get him back in and he manages to survive?

Damn my absurd thoughts. There is no goddamn pulse; I

had been giving him regular doses of death for four long weeks from the day I knew he existed. I looked up at the half-empty box of pills on the bathroom shelf, remembering the little letters written on the inside leaflet: 'aids upset stomach... but can induce miscarriage.'

Much appreciated. Abortion successful. I'll save the rest for an upset stomach.

I went back to examine him, he looked so beautiful and perfectly formed. I had had second thoughts a week into taking the pills daily without seeing a single drop of blood in my underwear, but I was told that pausing after a week of taking the pills would result in him coming into the world with a syndrome which would cause deformation of the skull and fingers, a syndrome whose name I could never pronounce.

I remember him on the palm of my hand, everything looked good and in place. From the tips of both arms sprouted small welded threads, like the fingers of a fist that was only just forming. I spread the delicate thighs with the tip of my finger to look in between, I couldn't guess the gender.

I left him wrapped in a handkerchief, took off my bloodstained clothes, washed and came back to him, I picked him up as I wondered what to do with him.

I didn't think I'd have to face getting rid of him again. I thought he was going to slide out of me invisibly, but he fell on the floor in front of my eyes. I was forced to look.

I thought I could grab him, wring him out, wash my hands, and then let the arms and the clenched fists and the little heart all disappear down the drain and forget him. But I couldn't kill him after I had seen him. Has my head become unscrewed again? I have *already* killed him. Or rather, with all my love and mercy, I saved him. He was going to die anyway; everyone dies in the end. I saved him from a lifetime in the bosom of Egypt, growing up, developing, working and aspiring to become an honourable citizen that I would no longer recognise.

The cawing of a crow crept into my ears that day; I

laughed, as I couldn't think of a cruder way to remind me that I should bury him now.

I went out onto the veranda towards the only potted plant I owned at the time, dug a hole his size in the dirt with my bare fingers, kissed his head, and made sure one last time that there was no pulse before I placed him in the hole and poured dirt on him.

I patted the surface level before going back to contemplating the plant pots surrounding me. That confusion had now passed, and the balcony had returned to resembling a garden. After the first time, it got easier. I had stashed dozens of boxes filled with the same pills in my drawer, just before the government took them off the market, releasing the link between increased sales and decreased fertility rates.

The voices from down below were getting louder and earplugs could no longer block them. I considered going back in, but I didn't want to leave my plants alone. What if some honourable citizen looked up and figured it out? Their voices were rising in a frenzy, not unlike the old madness that began with the First Leader's speech. I remember clearly how he began his speech by singing 'Egypt is my mother, the Nile is in my blood'. Then he stopped singing, just as a holographic scene appeared behind him, depicting soldiers slaughtering his opponents, their blood pooling onto the ground. He pointed to the blood with narrow eyes and a trembling voice: 'We slaughtered many citizens to search for the real Nile in their blood. Was there ever a physical Nile? No, not a physical one. The Nile was just a metaphor.' He raised his voice. His delivery changed from tender to enthusiastic as he cheered and waved.

'The Nile is just a metaphor, but Egypt will remain Mama… Egypt is Mama and I am Papa.'

I remember how, at the time, honourable citizens used to shout with the same frenzy: 'Egypt is Mama'. They were as honourable as they were insane, but their features hadn't all unified at that point.

That day, the world was reshaped, and the slogan 'Egypt is

Mama' started spreading everywhere, from school textbooks to shopping malls to public transport, to the fronts of passports before international travel was banned. The national symbol became a drawing of a fellah woman in natural colours, taking out her breasts from beneath her green robe, as citizens gathered around her, men and women, eager to feed from the teat. In elegant handwriting, written under it was: 'Egypt is Mama'.

Edicts started coming in thick and fast after that. It was decided that the Nile was a metaphor, but Egypt was a real mother and not a metaphor, so the government issued its decision that all children must be handed over to the state at birth, so that they could sink into the bosom of the state, suckle on the collective breast, and grow up as honourable citizens, sons of Egypt – all bearing the features of the leader, Papa, be they men or women. At first, I decided not to get married, knowing that Egypt would not accept any children born out of wedlock. But then a new edict was issued stating that children out of wedlock still belonged to Egypt.

The voices from down in the street were getting louder but they were no longer unified. I peered over the balcony wall to see: one of the rows had broken rank to form what looked like a circle of honourable citizens around a woman with a swollen belly. I studied her closely and realised that, despite her disguise, she was like me – with different features to the others. I saw her desperately shielding her belly with her arms, and watched as the circle narrowed around her as the screaming grew louder: 'Hand over the child to Mama!'

I sat on the floor, not daring to look, pressing my palms to my earplugs in vain. I looked at the plant pots that surrounded me. In one of them, it seemed as if something was growing out of the dirt, tiny fingers were trying to get out. I reached out and began picking and biting the leaves, one after another, until the plant was back to being a bare stick, and the tiny palm disappeared under the dirt.

Oral History of a Past, Obsolete and Forgotten

Yasmine El Rashidi

EVERYTHING I KNOW IS both firsthand and secondhand. Not firsthand as a witness, obviously – I'm not sure if anyone is still alive who was around at the time. Even if they are, and maybe this is something you've looked into, they couldn't have been more than a child when it happened. At the most, a young teenager. Still, it would be interesting to find them and see what kind of memories they have, the stories they might have heard as children and carried with them from that time. But, when I say 'firsthand', I mean I've seen documents and accounts from my grandmother – if that can be considered firsthand – recordings, her own testimony, untouched. Her more distilled, published accounts were, of course, secondhand, by everyone else's definition. But the separate notes that she kept, the recordings she made, unedited, the interviews she conducted with others, but also her own voice notes to herself – all of these felt to me like firsthand knowledge. When the archive came into my possession, it was already meticulously transcribed and organised. Still we – we, being a group of friends who'd all received personal archives from grandparents or relatives – we collectively went through everything and pooled resources to digitise them from their original formats. A few things were impossible to properly convert – small analogue audio tapes from recorders that I imagine were outdated even at the time – but we managed to convert most of it. But I should speak for myself, first, since the work is personal and private, even though it will eventually be uploaded to the *verse*.

My grandmother wasn't a central player in it; she wasn't what they call an activist, one of those who organised everything and who were on the streets ready to die for it. Thousands did die. Activists were like the programmers of their day. Back then – it was before *verse* – everything was in the flesh, on the streets. In person. It was a different moment in time, a different way of life. I can't imagine they would have known what everything would be like today, from what I've read of that time. They had physical telephones and computers that you had to actually control yourself. There was no conversion of thought into *verse*. The physical was the dominant. It's probably why there is so much in these personal archives, as they called them. There was no other way to store information, memories, content.

My grandmother was a writer. A published one. She was involved from the very beginning. There were these meetings, of maybe 30 or so people, in the flesh, and they were beginning to use what was then called Meta, or, I think maybe, Facebook. So they were beginning to use it to organise. It's hard to even imagine it now, of course.

For context, yes, let me explain: so we are speaking about Egypt here. I should have said this at the beginning. 100 years ago. A little bit more. The country was governed by a president. At the time, that particular president had been in office for 30 years, which was an overstepping of what I suppose was the typical duration of governance at the time. It seems obsolete now, to think of a country physically managed around government offices and a leader, a person.

ORAL HISTORY OF A PAST, OBSOLETE AND FORGOTTEN

Anyway, so this group of young organisers, they decided to plan for a series of physical protests on this one day, the 25th day of January in the year 2011. When you read back, there are all sorts of contradictory theories as to who was really behind this plan. The dominant narrative was that the USA, as it was called then, being a unified front, was a big driver behind this movement, which is maybe still the most widely held theory among historians of the time. But looking back, reading everything that remains, it's hard to say it was any one single entity. It seemed to be desired, deeply, on many fronts.

My grandmother was friends with a couple of the organisers, and people close to them, so on that morning, the 25th day of January, 2011, she headed out to what was then a square nearby, I forget the name. From the beginning, she was part of the protests, along with these two friends, although – as she writes – one of them was taken away by the state's thugs that morning, kidnapped as they were marching through the streets. That day turned into the largest protest in the country's history. By evening, tens of thousands of people were in the streets, all wanting the same thing, which, I suppose, they'd been wanting for years but had never been able to vocalise in such physical numbers before. Until then, they'd been too scared to, governments were in complete control and would have arrested and tortured them. But that day, it was different, even though it's still not entirely clear what exactly had changed to make it possible. It's hard for me to imagine what she, they, felt on that day. In one interview, she uses the word 'exhilaration', which I've found many others from the time use. I understand 'high', 'excited', but 'exhilarated' I can't imagine – or anything on that level. Of course, it's interesting to read any account from the time, given its connection to me.

A century ago isn't that far back and yet her life seems hard to envision: the labour of it, the day-to-day tasks. Having to actually make the physical effort to write everything down rather than being able to think it and convert it straight into *verse*. Everything was much more laboured – going to work, travelling, basic subsistence, the acquisition of things. And besides the day-to-day toiling, there was the endless, seemingly futile striving for a different kind of existence. At the time, they had no control over their own content; this government of theirs was constantly blocking, controlling, censoring, what they made. It's inconceivable to imagine that now. Inconceivable that a single person could have so much control over everything, from content to money, to what you could or couldn't buy, sell, bring into the country or out of it. Such a centralised system of power. My grandmother writes repeatedly about this one political prisoner, Alaa Abdel Fattah, who was younger than her, maybe ten years or so, and spent the larger part of his life in jail, precisely because of this centralisation. What's most interesting, to me, I think, is that people allowed this kind of authority to preside over them. You couldn't imagine someone assuming such absolute jurisdiction these days. And yet, I suppose at the time, there was just that one single physical world, no M, no verse, just the beginning of what were then NFTs. She writes a little about this shift into what they called 'the virtual', largely by way of her goddaughter, who was born in 2011 and functioned as her link to the future. She kept a record of her conversations with her goddaughter, who is called Malak, who boasts that she is in touch with 'the modern world' while her own 'godmother', who was technically her cousin but had been given guardianship of her, was 'out of touch'. Change was definitely afoot for that generation. My grandmother writes how this little girl – I'll just use her name from now on, Malak – was born already knowing how to use all forms of technology, and already aware, from before she could read or write, that AI and robots would soon control everything. In one entry, from 2018, she records Malak telling her that by the time she is grown up and has her own home, she wouldn't even have to get up to go to

ORAL HISTORY OF A PAST, OBSOLETE AND FORGOTTEN

the kitchen to make a sandwich. She would just say it out loud, or even think it, and the house droid would make it and bring it to her. My grandmother writes that Malak is absolutely certain of this, even at seven years old, even though it didn't exist as a reality then, to their knowledge. Of course she was right. What's most interesting about the archive, for me, is the shift that happened, that you can see in these documents as happening, between this event, that my grandmother was old enough to be involved in and young enough to be hopeful for the future about, and just a decade or so later, when all hope seems to have been lost for its aims, and a next generation had come up and started to chart a path to where we are now. This event, this revolution as they called it at the time, some of them, it was everything for my grandmother's generation. And yet for her goddaughter, it was nothing. She writes in her notes about the day this president – after he was ousted by the protests that she had been part of – years later, dies. On that morning, when she reads the news and comments aloud in disbelief that he is gone, Malak asks who it is she's talking about. The shift from one generation who knew no president but that one – my grandmother's first 30 years of life – to a new generation, so soon after, who didn't even know who he was. This was the beginning of where we are now, I think, when you chart the shift, and this new way of thinking. This little girl wanting AI to control her life. My grandmother's horror at the thought!

In as much as my grandmother's generation travelled a lot, if they had the resources, she definitely did. There's a note, from 2016 I think it is, she is in New York, she has been invited there to teach, and she spends a lot of her time, her spare time, going to art exhibitions and to the movies, which seems so alien a concept now, to have to physically travel to sit in a space to watch and have access to art. Anyway, she writes about an evening with her friend, a sculptor by the name of Iman Issa, and how they go to a screening of a film by Werner Herzog, where a programmer-computer-scientist-engineer (her description) talks about a future where you will be able to 'tweet a thought'. Twitter being a popular platform at the time, of course, before it then evolved to X. So there was a prophecy, among very specialised communities, of thought one day being transmittable across forms and media, but for most people, until this very young generation came about, such a reality was hard to conceive. That was the case for my grandmother. Although she herself moved in privileged and creative circles, among writers, artists, thinkers at the forefront of debates, her own generation was simply too old to tap into what eventually changed the world and their struggles. Her archive is filled with correspondences, from around the globe, with people like, well, Ahmed Naji, Maaza Mengiste, Negar Azimi, Gini Alhadeff, Alejandro Zambra. Forward-thinkers, and all writers of the world, even those forced into exile in the west. You get the sense, also, that there was a disconnect between the American view of the world, which you can find in her clippings, her obsessive filing of writing – a view that was insular, limited, self-referential – and the rest of the world's view of the world, which is in these rich correspondences.

One of my favourite moments, reading through all this material, and it has been years of work, is the moment when my grandmother in New York, once again, is invited to use the home of a wealthy patron, in what was then known as the West Village, around 4th and 10th Streets. It doesn't say why she's there, or how she ends up in an empty four-bedroom house alone, but she describes arriving, after flying for twelve hours from Egypt – it took that long – and venturing to the refrigerator to see if there's anything to eat. She finds a pint of ice cream, called Squeeze, about which she writes, 'You squeeze the container and it activates a warming mechanism, with warm chocolate sauce oozing through the centre and out of the top'. Apparently, my grandmother contemplates this for a long while, tempted to try it, famished from the long journey, but ultimately decides against opening the container, in case it's too expensive or rare to replace! Instead, she puts it back, goes upstairs, chooses a random bedroom, and gets into bed with her phone. She logs into her (then) Twitter account, which was her primary means of obtaining news from on-the-ground, and the first advertisement that pops up for her is for the ice cream downstairs! She writes, 'I think they're beginning to read our thoughts.' It was a scary notion at the time since you can tell she didn't know exactly who 'they' were, or what 'they' were doing with these thoughts. But I did laugh at that, imagining her in this huge house alone, seeing the advertisement pop up on her screen. She immediately tells a friend, a curator, Sarah, also from Egypt, who has just started doing a PhD in Boston (more on her later). Further into her papers – and it is a puzzle to piece together, going back and forth between everything – but later you learn that the imprisoned activist, Alaa Abdel Fattah, comes into her life through her friend Sarah. And the impact he has on her, on my grandmother, is because of his relationship to her goddaughter. He becomes a role model for Malak during a brief period when he is out of prison and on probation.

I have the sense, reading, that my grandmother never really recovers from the disappointments of 2011. Maybe not the political expectation that she and others had, but the way everything it opened up for her and her friends, was then shut down. You have the feeling that the world presented itself to them – embraced and courted them – because of this event, a heroism it seemed to suggest, but then quite quickly after sort of spat them out. In one of the published pieces, she writes about living in the shadow of it. I think she is referring to the 'exhilaration'. This word I can't let go of. It comes back to me. I've put that question out there, in *verse*: 'Has anyone felt exhilaration?' 'What is exhilaration?' 'What would be your closest experience of exhilaration?' 'Have you had any experience of it?' More than one question. Many questions. I've received thousands of responses. Perhaps this is the true legacy of my grandmother's archive, the emotional measure of what existed at the time, the diversity and variety of it. Compared to us now, this word, 'emotion', with all the spontaneity and circumstance it implies, seems outdated. And that's even to me, and I suppose I'm on the older end of the spectrum of the people you are speaking to about all this?

[End. 1.15pm, January 25th, 2111].

The Tanta White People Museum

Ahmed Naji

Translated by Rana Asfour

IT WAS WITH KAREN that I discovered the carefree joy of an embrace. Thus, as I stand at this wall, I am emboldened to write, for the first time, about the two of us, and the love that arrived rather late in life, but that couldn't have come at a more perfect time.

Most of the anecdotes displayed on the museum's wall, listed under the hashtag #success_stories, are rife with the challenges that white pioneers and their descendants have battled to overcome: marginalisation, stereotyping, the loss of opportunities, rights or property. In nearly all of them, white immigrants rose, despite the hands that pulled them down, to achieve 'success' – the end of the journey being jobs and assets that give them the illusion of security.

So, facing this wall, the white immigrant feels the need to apologise and seek validation. In most of the stories, the same essential message plays on a loop: *I am white; but despite this, I am successful, having contributed to this society and that civilisation.*

It was at this particular moment in my life, while I was

attending a conference in Neom for museums and heritage curators, basking in the fact that I was the country's first trans-white-woman museum director, when I received the news via a text message from our head of security. Suddenly, I became aware of the whispers and furtive glances of the attendees around the room. Those who knew me came forwards, palms extended to show me pictures and videos, and to ask the question, somewhere between gloating and consoling: 'What happened?'

Most just wanted to rub it in. I suspect there were some among them who wished the fire had consumed the whole of the museum and me along with it. As for myself, my utter shock and anger paralysed any rationality, and nullified my ability to say or see anything. I beat a swift retreat, apologising to my colleagues for my need to travel to Tanta and check on the state of the museum. I didn't even say goodbye to the organisers so as to avoid conversations that would only make me even angrier. I didn't want to lose my tongue in an outburst that would destroy even more than what was lost in the fire and bombing.

And yet, a senior figure in the field of museums and heritage, now one of His Majesty's advisors, put his dirty hand on my shoulder and asked me the galling question: 'Who might be behind this criminal act?'. I could only look at this person, who years before, when the project was nothing but a fledgling idea, had criticised it as promoting racism, hatred and discrimination. Egypt, he had argued at the time, 'did not see colour', and this project only sought to establish a fictional narrative built on its founder's personal identity disorder.

At the time, I hadn't officially registered as a woman yet, but everyone addressed me as such. Everyone that is, except this criminally-affiliated Arab-nationalist insect, who compelled me to swallow the insult by virtue of his power and position, and the fact that I knew I'd need his consent to release the funds required to restore whatever had just been destroyed.

I hopped on the first plane out from Neom to Mansoura, and from Mansoura Airport I took the Hyper Loop to Tanta.

*

I arrived in Tanta at ten in the evening. On the way home, the city was already draped in its familiar nightly attire, with crowds congregating in front of eateries, twinkling lights shining in red and green along Al-Nahhas Street, and teenagers skateboarding along the Grand Ali Bey Avenue. Police drones hovered in the sky, intermittently blinking with blue and red lights, warning those below that the security forces were forever vigilant, watchful and protective. Faced with this mundane ordinariness, I thought to myself that perhaps the sceptics were right, and no one in the city cared about a museum showcasing the history of the white race. But I knew my city too well. Like me, it feigned forgetfulness to the point where it could swallow its pain whole. In Tanta, everything appeared to be fine until it wasn't.

I arrived at my house and found two men installing a surveillance camera. 'For security,' one of them said without even looking at me. At that moment, the anger that had built up all day finally detonated: 'What are you both doing here? Who authorised the installation of this thing? By what law? Who is your superior?'

Just then, the front door opened to reveal a blonde policewoman, with hair bound in a tight braid, wearing a blue shirt that matched her official uniform, with a gun holstered under her armpit. Her smile felt like an invitation to take a nap. Her left eye was jet black, due to the smart security lens she was wearing. Her other eye was bright green, like an invitation to wake up already. She stepped aside to let me enter my own home and extended her hand towards me:

'Hi, Doctor. We've been trying to get hold of you since this morning. As you see, we had no option but to show up unannounced.'

Her presence in my apartment probably meant she already had permission to break in and search the place. I controlled myself and ran through a mental check of the legal steps I should start taking. The woman's face looked familiar to me. *I know this woman*, I thought. A few moments of silence descended on the four of us, then her face popped up in my memory banks.

'Karen. You're Karen, right?' I asked, as I extended my hand in return.

We had met several times at the Purple Rabbit bar on Ashraf Street, and had mutual friends.

'Major Karen Nur al-Huda,' she said.

She pressed her fingers to her badge and looked sternly at the two officers who were curious to see my anger dissipate so quickly on recognising their superior.

She asked me why I hadn't been answering my phone, so I explained I'd turned it off when I got on the plane and had forgotten to turn it back on again. She stood silent for a few seconds, and I wasn't sure if she was contemplating my answer or reading through my biometrics no doubt being displayed on the lens over her left eye. I noticed she was taller than me, didn't wear nail polish, and had a faint trace of red pencil on her lips.

At the bar, she had appeared more elegant, and I couldn't recall ever seeing her in trousers. She said that she hadn't come to interrogate me, at least not for the time being. The visit was to secure the house and assure my safety. It was difficult to predict their next step, she explained, given that they had issued threatening leaflets, denouncing me.

Finally, I thought, *they've come to check on me at last, and secure my home!* It had been seven years since I received my first threatening letter, and since then anonymously signed messages and small acts of vandalism had never stopped. But before I could say any of this, my bedroom door swung open and out stepped my mother.

What a hellish day of transgressions par excellence: not only had my life's work been the target of a terrorist attack, but my mother and the police were in my house without my permission or knowledge.

I didn't need to ask my mother what had brought her to my house, knowing her excuse would match that of the police: she'd tried to call but my phone was off, she got worried and decided to come by herself from Mansoura to Tanta to check on her only daughter – who, for the record, she still thinks of as her only son.

Mum didn't need to ask me how I was doing, but instead, launched into a monologue about my switched-off phone and her journey from Mansoura to here, all the time exaggerating her expressions of concern for me, for the benefit of our audience. Karen abruptly cut her off and turned to shake my hand. 'I think your day has been difficult enough. We're done for now. I'll contact you tomorrow to follow up on the investigation.'

As I shook Karen's hand, I noticed its long, attractive fingers, with healthy nails that shined without polish, then felt its iron grip. I heard the notification ping of my mobile indicating that she'd shared her contact details, and before she withdrew her hand from mine, she said: 'I'll see you soon. From now on, I'll be by your side.'

*

I couldn't bear the idea of sitting at home with my mother, so minutes after the police had left, I was out the door. In the dead of night, I headed toward the Saint al-Badawi Spiritual Centre. With each step, as the green dome of the white building loomed closer, my demons took flight, and the rhythm of my breathing slowed.

The Sayyid al-Badawi Mosque was demolished decades ago, and the Sayyid al-Badawi Centre for Spiritual and Social Activities built in its place. The basement of the building housed a library that included some of the rarest and most precious manuscripts and Islamic archaeological artefacts. Above it, on the ground floor, were the function halls dedicated to the rituals of the Qur'an, a washroom for the dead, as well as the corner where the funeral prayers took place. The next floor up housed a mosque – home to several hundred Muslim robots that you could rent from anywhere in the world to stand in your stead at Friday prayers. The mosque observed the Shafi'i school, which sanctioned that robots could indeed lead the masses in prayer. However, some elderly men and women still show up for prayers in person as an act of social solidarity.

I headed up, taking the stairs, rather than the elevator, all the way to the dome, on the top floor. I entered through a small door and, as happened every time I entered the hall, no sooner was I a few steps in, than I was enveloped in calm and tranquillity. I came here to reflect on how far we'd come in the last hundred years. The mere existence of this centre and its transformation were testaments to our ability to achieve the message and the dream, the universality of the calling and our ability to save humanity from ignorance, fanaticism and violence.

The dome enclosed a white circular hall, in which wooden chairs were arranged in a ring-shaped circle. A gold-painted, wooden pedestal rose from the centre of the ring, where Saint Badawi's green turban sat on display. As it caught the light, it emitted an iridescent green that filled the white space with serenity, inviting calm and stillness to flow and spread within my wandering spirit.

Despite not having a God to pray to, I sat across from the Badawi's turban, and recited the line of poetry engraved at the

THE TANTA WHITE PEOPLE MUSEUM

base: *The dome of our master and guardian, light up when the people call; how glorious are the banners with each and every visit.* I closed my eyes and repeated it 33 times, oblivious to how smoothly the hymn of the Grand Sufi Night rolled off my tongue, my body swaying to its melody, as the faint echo of my tempered chant enfolded me in a cloud of repose.

★

A hundred years ago, Tanta was neither relevant nor a global symbol of peaceful coexistence between different religions and races. Tanta was nothing but a regional city wracked by sectarian conflicts, shaken by church bombings and terrorist attacks, drowning in a quagmire of ignorance and the lousy rebirth of the *mawlid*.

All that's left of that ancient time is Sayyid Al-Badawi's turban. A century-old remnant from a time when the world fell into decline with the onset of the Arab Spring and the January Revolution, whose values undermined the legitimacy of the past and made way for a new Arab-Islamic world, that carried the torch of change.

The first twenty years were the most difficult and frustrating; The country oscillated between revolution and civil war until salvation finally came with the emergence of Karama, a visionary organisation with a blueprint for a new reality, in which borders between Arab countries would fall away, markets and tax systems unify, and management models decentralise. Only one enemy was identified as a threat to this political project: the Gulf's royal families.

These days, no one likes to talk about the Half-Decade of Blood; the years in which Karama released the lists of names, photos and addresses of all royal dynasties in the region, from the tribal families of the Gulf, to those from a military backcloth in North Africa and the Levant, asking all honest and free people to liquidate them wherever they could be found, to nationalise their wealth, to deceive, and conspire against them, if not in deed then at least in their hearts. Those years finally ended after long negotiations, and the emergence of a new model for Arab constitutional monarchies, united under the banner of the Last King of the Sulaymaniyah Dynasty, over what became known as the Arab Kingdom.

This monarchy arose as an alliance between liberal capitalists and right-wing Islamist 'centrists', and forged initiatives to transform Arab markets, open borders, unify tax systems, and strengthen local governance. It appeared that history was finally in favour of the Arabs and Muslims after centuries of humiliation, disenfranchisement and ignorance. However, these changes encouraged the emergence of right-wing parties in the West whereby Europe and America re-embraced their innate white Nazi identity. When the leader of the American Evangelical Church, Ivanka Trump, became president of the United States, things got even more complicated, especially when she joined with other Western countries to repudiate climate change. Anyone who acknowledged climate change was imprisoned, and all environmental research centres – branded the work of the devil – were shut down. Trump even announced the date of Judgement Day and the Second Coming if she lost the next election.

Soon, though, the planet had had its fill of Nazi absurdity. The pace of climate change accelerated, and large swathes of Europe and America were drowned; the rising sea swallowed the state of Louisiana, while the melting ice caps put parts of Sweden and Denmark under water. Then, the epidemic hit. Despite the fact that according to scientists, the virus had lain dormant, frozen in the Arctic until the meltdown resurrected it, the head of the American Evangelical Church still chose to call it the African Virus.

The Arab and Islamic peoples joined efforts with China, and other countries in Asia and Africa to develop a vaccine against the virus, and to control the severity of climate change, while Western countries refused to help them.

Ultimately, a team of scientists led by Dr. Arundhati Roy managed to create a vaccine against the virus, but with a side effect on those with fair skin, causing their skin to darken, from white to brown and in some cases black. Although this transformation increased people's immunity against skin cancer and other diseases, many white people refused to be vaccinated, regarding it as an infringement on their cultural specificity and the values of Western Civilisation. Or, as the French President, Marine Le Pen put it: 'This is not a vaccine, but a weapon. A biological threat to the values of the French Republic.'

The result was an environmental and humanitarian catastrophe for white people. Average birth rates plummeted by a third and death rates doubled. Anyone opposed to the status quo was subjected to abuse, forcing the best Western minds to migrate to the Arab and Islamic countries that received them with open arms.

My grandfather and his family emigrated from Germany. After years of arbitrary flash floods and torrential downpours, the German government announced that it could no longer afford to sustain them, offering to relocate them instead to higher, mountainous areas. However, my grandfather received an offer to work in Egypt at the Delta Drug and Vaccine Company, so we emigrated. My father was three years old when he arrived with my grandfather in Mansoura. He later moved to Tanta to study architecture, after which he decided to settle down in the city.

My family were among the lucky ones. Not only were they educated and skilled, but they were also fortunate enough to encounter Egyptians and Muslims who treated them with respect, irrespective of their white skin. Sadly, this was not the experience of millions of other white people who migrated, legally or illegally, to the South, many perishing at sea, many others forced to adopt cultural norms contrary to their beliefs and values. White Americans, for example, were forced to acquire free health insurance, which they regarded as contrary to the teachings of Christ and the American Constitution. Furthermore, white history was being rewritten by the dominant Islamic powers and factions. The Karama movement, in particular, with its fascist and nationalist tendencies, played a systemic role, through various institutions, in erasing all evidence of white people's achievements. They re-defined the Nineteenth and Twentieth Centuries into ones ravaged by World Wars, famine and nuclear bombings, and held white people responsible for all of it, as if the oil and gas they often fought over wasn't now propelling the Arabs, and the Karama movement especially, into the future.

On my way out of the Sayyid al-Badawi Centre, I stopped in front of the foundation plaque, extended my hand to the carved marble, and traced my fingers along the name of my father – the architect who designed this building, and the visionary politician who transformed Tanta into a city that now stands for peaceful coexistence between diverse intellectual and ethnic backgrounds.

*

I arrived at the museum weary, puffy-eyed, and questioning everything I'd ever tried to do. I had only myself to blame, and with thoughts of the forthcoming emergency meeting of the Board of Trustees, I could not rule out stepping down and tendering my resignation.

My health monitor alerted me that my blood sugar was low – I'd only had a coffee and a protein shake that morning, along with my hormonal meds, so I decided to postpone any decision until my body chemistry had stabilised. I would not step down, or at least I would not consider it, today. I ordered a vegetarian lunch from the museum cafeteria which, surprisingly, wasn't affected by the explosion or the fire although the museum was closed to the public, it cont: to serve staff.

Feeling slightly better, I met with the museum's he security who presented me with the official report. Appa: a bomb had been placed under the interactive Steve Ba statue, whereas the fire had started in the Spiritual Herit: White People hall.

How do we know? Well, the security cameras had c the terrorist, all clad in black and wearing a pig appearing in the corridor leading to the History of \ Resistance Movements hall. The cameras didn't capture \ the terrorist had come from, which meant that, most they had been tampered with. The terrorist carries two in this footage: one strapped to the back, and the dangled from one hand. Once inside, the individual perfectly still, as if to bid a final farewell to the exhibits, l placing the bag at the foot of the Bannon statue.

The perpetrator then makes their way to the other (the museum, to the hall of The Spiritual History of ` People where they take out two plastic bottles from th and spray their contents over the exhibits. The camer: shows the same individual brandishing a lighter w drawing of the defunct European Union flag. Once the is ignited, the lighter sails through the air towards the soaked exhibits. Everything goes up in flames and the te disappears as if into thin air.

None of these exhibits were damaged. As soon as tl started, the sirens along with the fire extinguishing s kicked in. But just as the security personnel and the firefi; teams headed to the fire there, the bomb exploded (opposite side of the museum, blowing up the Resistanc(destroying its artefacts, and causing major damage to : other adjoining rooms.

As I was reviewing the reports, Karen walked in

office. Her golden locks were let down this time and, in the morning light, her head appeared bathed in a golden halo. She wasn't wearing a security lens, and when our eyes met, I was swept up in an erotic whirlwind of energy. She said she had come to chat before the formal interrogation, at the police station, at five.

I got up from behind the desk, shook her hand, and offered her a seat on the leather sofa, seeing as it was an informal visit. I wasn't surprised by my change of mood on seeing her, because I wanted her. It wasn't a sultry yearning or a fleeting seductive fancy, I wanted to belong to her. Only later would she admit that she had long craved my attention, had been delighted to be assigned my case, and that it was in that moment, when she'd stepped into my office, that she had felt truly seen.

But then, she asked why, on the day of the attack, only one security guard had been on duty to man both gates of the museum? Why had the CCTV room been unguarded?

'A shrinking budget!' For years, I had been appealing to various foundations and entities to increase their funding for the museum, I explained. It had been the main reason I'd been in Neom. Three months ago, federal funding to the museum had been substantially cut, leaving the museum largely reliant on 'tributes' from the Sulaymaniyah Royal Palace, which meant we didn't have enough funds to hire guards or pay for comprehensive security.

She nodded sympathetically, then told me that she believed it was an inside job: a lone wolf or someone in collaboration with an individual or group on the outside, intent on sending a message that she suspected was buried under what remained of the White Resistance Movements exhibit.

Then she asked me: 'Who would want to blow up this particular department?'

THE TANTA WHITE PEOPLE MUSEUM

★

Ever since I can remember, I never felt I belonged to Tanta, or the Arab Kingdom of Sulaymaniyah. This pained my father no end, who, in his later years, finally admitted that he only entered politics, and burned himself out in it, to create a space and a home to which I could lay the claim of belonging.

As a teenager, I travelled to Germany to find a lake where my grandfather's city had once stood. The country had fragmented into a federation of minor states and emirates run by large, industrial corporations that worked the population under miserable conditions – being a more affordable alternative to costly robots.

I was always considered a foreigner in Tanta. I suffered bullies and was labelled 'soft' because of my fair hair and blue eyes. Isolated from the outside world, I sought friendship and community in virtual reality, and when I turned nineteen, I finally confided in my father how I felt trapped in a body that was not mine, that I wanted to transition.

I left Tanta and Shady behind me as I moved to Dubai as Sherry, returning five years later as Dr. Shereen. On the day of my return, my father took me to visit the Saint Sayyid al-Badawi Centre for the first time which hadn't yet officially opened to the public. We stood together in that hall where he confessed he might have to leave at any moment.

It occurred to me that he might be ill or dying, but he explained that fascist and fundamentalist divisions were growing on both sides. White immigrants were blaming People of Colour and Arabs for all their suffering, accusing them of exploitation and getting rich on the destruction of their homelands. This was old news. What was new was that they had launched campaigns of intimidation that involved sending serious threats to white politicians – like my father – who they accused of selling out. On the other side, extremist groups linked to the emerging Kemet Party, were demanding the deportation of white people back to their sinking countries.

All the major political parties were unhappy with the concept of the Sayyid al-Badawi Centre, which they regarded as standing as an infringement on values, and cultural specificity, promoting and imposing the values and culture of white immigrants.

That day I learned, from Baba, that the public spaces, including the market place, were spaces that forced people to accept one another, to work and cohabitate, in peace, and that should we hand over those spaces to the bigots, then they will come to our homes and before long we won't even have them.

*

In place of an explanation, I offered Karen a tour of the museum. She asked me questions about my work history and the nature of my role and responsibilities at the museum, and quickly I found myself sharing things that I hadn't told anyone before: about my immigrant grandfather; about my 'khawaga' father's estrangement in Tanta, despite never knowing any other homeland; and about the time in my mid-30s, right after my father died, when I'd quit my job at the university in Dubai, forfeiting all the accolades and recognition I'd achieved in the art world, deciding instead to return to Tanta.

I told her how, initially, I hadn't known what it was I was looking for. I was going around town and the nearby villages, often on a bike, looking for a reason to justify my return. If the weather turned, I'd head into the city museum and spend hours trawling its archives. It was there that I stumbled on a story, in *al-Lata'if,* an illustrated magazine, from March 1917, profiling an altruistic endeavor in Tanta that supported and provided shelter for European orphans who had lost their parents during WWI. Accompanying the report was a picture of three blond children hunched over their desks, engrossed in writing. What the report would reveal was that those children were never told that their parents had perished in Europe, but instead were encouraged to write to them until the time that they could finally be reunited.

The story haunted me. I was fascinated with how this orphanage, through the exercise of writing, had trained its pupils to maintain hope. I returned to the archives, and collected everything I could – from paper suppliers and antiques dealers – relating to that period and that orphanage. Soon, the multiple layers of Tanta began to peel away, and I realised that white refugees, like my family, who had escaped wars, floods, and epidemics, had always been part and parcel of this city, their stories woven into its fabric. That's when the idea for the Tanta White People Museum was born, initially as an exhibition of the hidden history of white people I'd uncovered in Tanta, specifically; then, as the project developed, it became more about restoring respect for the history and culture of white people generally, after decades of demonisation. I passionately relayed all this to Karen as I pointed out the various artefacts on display.

'No race, in the history of mankind, has ever been so severely distorted, misjudged and condemned like that of the white race. It's been labelled imperialist, and racist, as if it was somehow inherently evil. Its historical achievements have been sidelined, and attributed instead to slaves, colonised peoples and immigrants. This project reconsiders the great ideas that white minds have produced, such as the Catholic Church, the American Constitution, the confinement of dangerous ideas within the walls of academia and anthropology departments, debt, compound interest, and other great ideas.'

*

The most valuable items in the museum are not exhibits that can be blown up or set on fire, but rather what we've preserved in the cloud, and presented on what we call 'The Wall'. In the history of the white race, nothing has been more central than the erection of walls; without them there would be no white culture

It's well known that as soon as any group of white people come together, the first thing they do is build fences and raise any existing walls. Later, tales and legends would propagate, on the far side of these walls, about a lurking dark presence threatening danger and harm. This sense of menace from behind the wall is what pushed the white race to continually innovate. Its most important achievements – from the smart bomb to democracy – all appeared from its side of a wall, to defend it, or to compensate for an absence of wall.

When we established the museum, our first thought was for a wall that would convey white people's passion for building up and then knocking down these structures. But walls are also homes for graffiti, for whispered confessions and hidden secrets. Our electronic wall is a screen about ten metres long, connected to servers that feed into an archival system. White immigrants are invited to upload their personal photos, videos, audio recordings, and texts documenting their experiences and personal stories, rendering the wall an interactive, valuable and diverse archive.

When I received word about the terrorist's arrest and her subsequent trial date, my immediate reaction was to document it all. However, when I began writing and collecting reports and photos to upload on to The Wall, it dawned on me that the purpose behind The Wall's inception had never been to catalogue major incidents, but rather, as a space for independent narratives of stranded immigrants with nowhere to belong. As I looked back on all that had taken place, I still regarded the bombing and burning of the museum as despicable acts of terrorism, but, I acknowledged that they also brought me love, and Karen, and above all, they made me realise that sadness and disenfranchisement need not be white people's one and only narrative.

THE TANTA WHITE PEOPLE MUSEUM

The day I returned to the museum, after the bombing, and met with Karen, I'd been exhausted, thinking I had reached that point where I no longer had the fight in me, that it was time I withdrew and surrendered. I felt like I was no longer the right person to be in charge. That a dark-skinned, Muslim man with the right personality and qualifications would better fill the leadership position, someone who would command respect from the police, state agencies, and the institutes of culture and heritage.

But, as I stood with Karen in front of The Wall that day, I felt the resurgence of a passion that had left me years before. Her interest in my story, her questions and comments enveloped me in a sense of belonging and companionship, of a bond to something bigger and more powerful than the two of us.

When we reached the History of White Resistance hall, where the explosion had taken place, we stood amid the ashes as I explained to Karen how, a hundred years ago, western civilisation had witnessed the emergence of resistance and liberation movements that had come in defence of the white narrative, only to be cancelled, stigmatised and marginalised. After listening to my account, Karen then asked why the terrorist had chosen Bannon's statue to plant his bomb.

Bannon, I told her, was the last of the great white prophets. He was a symbol of white resistance for his stalwart championing of white heritage, playing a vital role in the emergence of many resistance movements that rallied against illegal immigrants and the dictatorship of authorities in charge of controlling epidemics. I explained to Karen that the exhibits in the hall, where the Bannon statue now lay in pieces, focused on reviving oppressed and marginalised narratives, celebrating the legacy of proud, white thinkers and theorists, and worked to counter the propaganda of People of Colour and Muslims, such as Jordan Peterson, and the descendants of the martyr St. Trump. It took no stretch of the imagination to conceive why radical fundamentalist groups would be intent on destroying these symbolic artefacts.

Karen had stood in the middle of the room, each hand buried deep in the pockets of her jacket, taking in what remained of the walls and the soot-covered ruins of the exhibition. Save for the rays of natural light pouring in from the large windows, forming square patches in several places on the hall's floor, the room was in semi-darkness. In the middle of one of those squares of light stood Karen, who suddenly turned towards me. Our eyes locked sending an involuntary shiver to course through me.

'We caught the culprit,' she said. 'I didn't want to tell you before the official press conference at the police headquarters today. We haven't announced anything yet since we're still searching for her accomplices.'

'Who?'

'Jameela Fox,' she said.

'Impossible. Why would she?' I asked, thinking how I'd only hired her five months before.

'We're not sure yet but what's obvious is that she was recruited by a radicalised white queer group, most likely one of the Stray Wolves. Many of this new generation of white youth harbour a deep contempt for their white ancestry, and only seem to take pleasure in self-flagellation.'

In response, I raised my face to the ceiling, trying to capture the warmth of the descending beam of light. I could feel the sting of repressed tears push against my eyelids.

'Are you OK?' she asked.

'Can you believe I haven't cried since I got the news? How is it possible that I can't find a single shoulder to cry on? Loneliness is such a tiresome business.'

When I lowered my head, she was standing right in front of me, her arms open wide. I walked into her embrace and there I remain.

About the Authors

Mansoura Ez-Eldin is an award-winning author of ten books, including *Walks in Shanghai* winner of the 2021 Ibn Battuta Prize for travel literature, and *Emerald Mountain* winner of 'Best Arabic Novel' at the 2014 Sharjah International Book Fair (SIBF). Her writing has appeared, among other places, in *Beirut39*, Granta, *New York Times*, *A Public Space* and *The Neue Zürcher Zeitung*. Ez-Eldin is an Honorary Fellow in the University of Iowa's International Writing Program.

Belal Fadl (1974-) studied journalism at Cairo University, before working for prominent newspapers, magazines and television networks across the Arab world. He has written sixteen movies and five TV's series. In 2009, he won 'Best Screenplay' for his film *Boltya el Ayma* at Egypt's 15th National Film Festival. He has written four collections of short stories as well as fifteen books of satire, culture, and travel. His debut novel *Umm Mimi* (*Mimi's Mother*) was longlisted for the 2022 Arab Booker Prize. One of his stories won the *Arablit* Magazine Award, while another was shortlisted. He left Egypt in 2014, and continues to write in New York City.

Ahmed Fakharany (1981-) was born in Alexandria and worked at *Shorouk* and *el-Badil* newspapers, before establishing himself as a novelist. His fourth novel *Bayaset Al-Shawam* (*Syrian Square*) won the 2021 Sawiris Foundation Award in the novels/emerging writers category.

ABOUT THE AUTHORS

Michel Hanna (1977-) is a novelist and short story writer. His work has been published in many Egyptian newspapers, magazines and websites such as *Al-Dustour* newspaper and *Aladdin's* magazine for children. His most recent novels include *Al Sahera wel Kalb* (*The Witch and the Dog*, 2021), and *Gissr El Digital* (*The Digital Bridge*, 2019) which was long listed for Sheikh Zayed Prize for Child Literature in 2021. His short story collections include *Al Ganeb Al Mozlem Min El Qamar* (*The Dark Side of the Moon*, 2008) and *Ana wa ana* (*Me and I*, 2012) a graphic novel for adults.

Camellia Hussein (1986-) graduated from the Faculty of Arts, Cairo University. She published her first novel, *Hide and Seek* in 2023 as part of the Aswat wa Khutoot Crime Fiction Workshop, organised by Storytel.

Heba Khamis (1987-) is an Egyptian writer, working as a journalist and creative writing tutor and mentor, specialising in short fiction. She has published two collections: *From a Window Overlooking the Square* (2011), which won the Culture Palace Central Prize, *Zar* (2017), which won the 2019 Sawiris Cultural Prize, and the *American Residences*, which was shortlisted for the same award in 2023.

Mohamed Kheir is a novelist, poet, short story writer, journalist, and lyricist. His short story collections *Remsh Al Ein* (2016) and *Afarit Al Radio* (2011) both received The Sawiris Cultural Award, and *Leil Khargi* (2001) was awarded the Egyptian Ministry of Culture Award for poetry. His second novel *Eflat Al Asabea/Slipping* (Kotob Khan, 2018/Two Lines Press, 2021) has been translated into English by Robin Moger.

Nora Nagi (1987-) was born in Tanta and is the author of five novels: *Pana* (2015), *The Wall* (2016), *The Basha Girls* (2017) and *Spectres of Camelia* (2020), which won the Haqqi Award, and *Years of Running in Place,* as well as a collection of interviews, *Women Writers and Unity* (2019, all Dar Al-Shorouk).

Ahmed Naji (1985-) is a writer and journalist who was awarded the PEN/Barbey Freedom to Write Award in 2016. He is the author of two novels *Rogers* (2007) and *Use of Life* (2014). Nagi was arrested after an excerpt from the latter novel was published in *Akhbar al-Adab*. He was sentenced to two years in jail for violating public morality. This second novel has been translated into Italian and English. His first collection of short stories, *Siniora* was published in 2016 by Merit, and the title story featured in Comma's *The Book of Cairo* (2019).

Yasmine El Rashidi is a regular contributor to *The New York Review of Books*, and an editor of the Middle East arts quarterly *Bidoun*. She is the author of *The Battle for Egypt: Dispatches from the Revolution* and *Chronicle of a Last Summer: A Novel of Egypt*, and was a Fellow at the Institute for Ideas and Imagination in Paris. She lives in Cairo.

Azza Sultan (1974-) is an award-winning journalist, screenwriter, author and occasional film director. Her children's books include *The Dove's Strange Journey* (1998), and *The Merry Animals* (1999). She has published four short story collections, including *Imra'a talid rajulaan yushbibuk* (*A Woman Gives Birth to a Man Who Resembles You*, GACP, 1999), and a novel *Tadribat fi il-Qaswa* (*Exercises in Cruelty*, 2014).

Ahmed Wael is a writer and scriptwriter, specialising in TV. He is a graduate of the Clockwork Temptation writers workshop alongside writer, Mohamed Amin Radi and film critic, Ahmed Shawky and is best known for *Words on Paper* (2014), and *Homes Have Secrets* (2015). He also co-wrote the series *The Journey* (2018) with Amr El Daly.

About the Translators

Maisa Almanasreh is a freelance translator and interpreter with a masters degree in Business and Public Service Interpreting and Translation at the University of Leeds. She is originally from Palestine and is now based out of Lisbon, Portugal.

Rana Asfour is the Managing Editor at *The Markaz Review*, as well as a freelance writer, book critic and translator. Her work has appeared in such publications as *Madame Magazine*, *The Guardian* and *The National*. She chairs the TMR English-language BookGroup.

Raphael Cohen is a professional translator and lexicographer. His most recent publications are the novel *Guard of the Dead* by George Yaraq (2019) *Madness of Despair* by Ghalya Al Saeed (2021) plus a selection of Ahmed Morsi's poetry *Poems of Alexandria and New York*. He contributed to *Blade of Grass, An Anthology of New Palestinian Poetry* (ed. Naomi Foyle, 2017) and has translated a number of novels including Mona Prince's *So You May See* (AUC) and Ahlem Mosteghanemi's *Bridges of Constantine* (Bloomsbury). He is a contributing editor of *Banipal*.

Raphael Cormack is Assistant Professor of Arabic at Durham University. He is a translator, editor and author with a PhD in modern Arabic literature. He is the co-editor of Comma's *The Book of Khartoum* (2016), with Max Shmookler, and editor of *The Book of Cairo* (2019). He is the author of *Midnight in Cairo* (2021), a book about the female entertainers of early 20th Century Egypt.

ABOUT THE TRANSLATORS

Basma Ghalayini is a literary translator from Gaza. She has translated short stories for the Commonwealth Writers, Maalboret, Deep Vellum Press and Comma Press. She was the editor of *Palestine + 100* (Comma, 2019), and co-editor of the special Palestinian edition of *Strange Horizons* (2021).

Mohammed Ghalayini worked for two years as reporter for New York-based Free Speech Radio News in Gaza and as a presenter on Palestine Satellite Channel, conducting and translating live interviews and reports, and whilst in Gaza has volunteered regularly as a translator for the Union of Health and Work Committees. He was a contributing translator to *The Book of Khartoum,* and *Palestine + 100* (Comma, 2016 and 2019) and currently works in the field of air quality in the UK.

Mayada Ibrahim is a literary translator based in Queens, New York, with roots in Khartoum and London. She works between Arabic and English. Her translations have been nominated for the Pushcart Prize and published by Willows House in South Sudan, Foundry Editions, Archipelago Books, Dolce Stil Criollo, and 128 Lit. She is the managing editor at Tilted Axis Press.

Elisabeth Jaquette is a translator from Arabic and Executive Director of the American Literary Translators Association (ALTA). Her translation of *Minor Detail* by Adania Shibli (Fitzcarraldo/New Directions) was a finalist for the National Book Awards and longlisted for the International Booker Prize. Other translations include *Thirteen Months of Sunrise* by Rania Mamoun (a finalist for the Warwick Prize for Women in Translation) and *The Queue* by Basma Abdel Aziz (nominated for the Best Translated Book Award and TA First Translation Prize).

ABOUT THE TRANSLATORS

Andrew Leber is an assistant professor in the Department of Political Science and Middle East & North Africa Studies at Tulane University in New Orleans. His academic writing has appeared in journals such as *Politics & Society* and *Foreign Affairs*, while his occasional translations of Arabic literature have appeared in outlets such as AGNI online, the *New Statesman*, *Jadaliyya*, *Guernica*, *ArabLit Quarterly*, and several previous Comma Press anthologies.

Robin Moger is a translator of Arabic to English currently based in Cape Town, South Africa. His translations of prose and poetry have appeared in *Blackbox Manifold*, *The White Review*, *Tentacular*, *Asymptote*, *Words Without Borders*, *The Johannesburg Review of Books*, *The Washington Square Review* and others. He has translated several novels and prose works into English including Mohamed Kheir's *Slipping* (Two Lines), Iman Mersal's *How To Mend* (Kayfa ta), Nael Eltoukhy's *The Women of Karantina* (AUC Press) and Youssef Rakha's *The Crocodiles* (Seven Stories).

Majd Abu Shawish is a translator and interpreter based in Sheffield, originally from Nuseirat, Gaza Strip. He has an MA in Global Political Economy from the University of Sheffield. He received the 'Liam Holden Memorial Prize'. He has previously translated for *The Guardian*.

Paul Starkey was, until his retirement in 2012, Professor of Arabic and Head of the Arabic Department at Durham University, UK, and Co-Director of the Centre for the Advanced Study of the Arab World. Until 2018, he was also Vice President of the British Society for Middle Eastern Studies. Paul has published widely in the field of modern Arabic literature, as well as on Middle Eastern travel literature; he was co-editor of *The Encyclopedia of Arabic Literature* (1998) and author of *Modern Arabic Literature* (EUP, 2006). He has also translated many novels and short stories into English.